Beth Locke, a talented athlet freshman year of college when she meт тne beautiful Anne Stetson. Through their passion of running, they developed a close relationship that would blossom into a love so deep that the thought of living without each other was almost unbearable.

Their story is filled with moments of desire, excitement, and exhiliirating firsts, especially for the naïve, yet eager Beth Locke. If you remember the feelings of first love, this book will stir those memories and help you feel like you're living it all over again.

Hope you enjoy it!.
Susanne Gabel Pierson

Dedication

This book is dedicated to my wonderful wife and best friend, Jude Lesher, who was willing to sleep with the light on so I could continue typing late at night. Her endless supply of potato chips, Kit Kats, Diet Coke, and Michelob Ultra, along with her sweet encouragement, helped me finally finish this book.

This book is also dedicated to the women in my past who I was privileged enough to share my love with. Those memories will remain in my heart forever.

Acknowledgements

I couldn't have completed this book without the brilliance and patience of my editor in chief, Susan Graves. I can't thank you enough.

I'm forever grateful to my wonderful friend, Sue Sisto, for providing me an extra pair of eyes to find the mistakes that I was blind to.

A special thanks to my sister, Dr. Judith Pierson, for her consistent loving support and validation.

Sincere thanks to my model, Carol "Cub" Stratton, for being kind enough to lend me her runner's body so I could create some of the images of my main character, Beth Locke.

Thank you Jan Johnson, for becoming my new Coach Ryan.

Table of Contents

CHAPTER ONE

Beth

Beth was already breathing heavily as she ran along a flat stretch of gravel road. There was a steep hill approaching and she dreaded the idea of keeping that same pace as she began to climb. Several times she thought she might surrender to its incline. Her legs felt heavy and her breathing grew labored. She could no longer ignore the stitch in her side, but she still refused to slow her pace. She was fiercely determined to reach the top and regarded the discomfort as motivation. With only a few more strides to its peak, Beth could almost feel those throbbing muscles relax and that struggle for air subside. As she came over the top and started down, her breathing became effortless, and she allowed her mind to drift freely. She kept pace to the rhythm of her sneakers crunching the loose gravel beneath them as she enjoyed the quiet countryside. It was a beautiful autumn afternoon. The air was filled with the aroma of drying leaves and dying grass. Even the smell of the cow pasture, when the breeze didn't make it too strong, was rather pleasant. As she ran gracefully down the final hill of the college cross country course, her body recovered quickly. What was just work was now like play.

Beth was about five feet seven inches tall. Her body was thin and muscular. The muscles in her legs were noticeably well defined, and when she wore a sports bra, it revealed the "six pack" that she had earned with hours of training and thousands of crunches. Just by looking at her, you knew she was an athlete.

Beth called herself a "mixed bag of nationalities" and her appearance reflected that. She was part Italian, Eastern European, and Brazilian. She could speak some Portuguese because her Brazilian grandmother made sure of it by speaking to Beth only in her native language. Beth's hair, which was in a ponytail, was a dark brown. Her near perfect looking white teeth stood out against her bronze skin. Except for a small scar through her right eyebrow, that she got from falling off her bike as a child, her face was unblemished. Her dark brown eyes were emphasized by her thick, long lashes. She wore no makeup and didn't need any to highlight her already appealing features. Throughout her childhood, Beth, who never had a problem sharing her thoughts, conveyed assertively that she was proud to be a tomboy and promised herself that she would never let anyone talk her into wearing "stupid makeup". Now as an eighteen-year-old college freshman, it appeared that she had lived up to her promise. According to Beth, keeping a promise was one of the most important things in life.

Beth's attention soon focused on another runner coming towards her. She could almost feel the pain this

9

runner would experience climbing the hill that she was so easily descending. From a distance she could barely make out what the runner looked like but was impressed by the running style. It was that of an experienced runner. Suddenly, Beth realized the approaching runner was a girl. Without a thought she picked up her pace and tried to look smooth. She grew more nervous as they approached each other. The other runner was slender like Beth but was several inches taller. Her long legs were making quick and steady strides unbroken by the hill's steep incline. There were strong indications that this young woman worked outside during the summer, because her skin was still tan, and her blond hair looked as though it had been bleached by the summer sun. Beth figured she was probably a lifeguard. When they were just a yard or so apart, Beth looked up into a pair of stunning light blue eyes and a generous welcoming smile. Beth spoke first as they were about to pass each other. "Hi...I like your sneakers," she blurted out jokingly because she had just noticed they had the same ones.

"Well thank you," the young woman smiled. "I like yours too," she yelled back. Beth ran down the trail, blushing with embarrassment.

"Oh Christ, I can't believe I just said that!" she mumbled to herself. While she continued to reprimand herself for looking like an "idiot", she had the urge to turn around and watch her run. She enjoyed watching good runners. There was something delightful about the way their bodies moved. To her, it was the combination of grace and strength. Without changing her pace, she managed to turn her head far enough so she could watch her. It was impressive. Suddenly, the runner glanced back. She caught Beth watching her. Beth quickly turned and pretended she was looking at something in the field.

"Shit!" she uttered. "She must think I'm crazy." She picked up her pace and quickly turned off the road.

As she ran the final mile around the main campus, a yellow convertible Mustang with the top down, pulled up beside her. In it sat a rather plump young woman with bleached blonde hair. It was Chris, her roommate.

"Want a ride?" Chris shouted.

"No thanks. I've gone this far. I think I need to finish the rest."

"Won't all that running make you manly?" Chris asked seriously.

"I hope not," Beth said laughing.

"Me too!" Chris called out as she drove off, waving goodbye.

Beth and Chris were both freshmen and had been assigned to room together. They hadn't been roommates for even a month, but Beth sensed they would never become close friends. Chris was the type who spent a half hour putting on her makeup each morning and another half hour deciding what to wear. Her only interests seemed to be the soap operas and boyfriends. Although their lifestyles and interests were vastly different, they treated each other with fairness and respect. So far they hadn't had any problems, but Beth wasn't sure if she wanted to room with Chris next semester. She thought Chris might feel the same way. The only problem was that Beth hadn't met anyone yet, that she would feel comfortable enough to ask if they would like to share a room with her. Not being surrounded by a large group of friends was an unfamiliar feeling for her. In high school, Beth had more friends than she could count. She was comfortable with who she was and felt no need to belong to any one group of students. Perhaps, it was the combination of her family's values and her own self-confidence, which helped her be nonjudgmental and kind to just about everyone. It was likely that those traits, had earned her the respect and admiration of the other students and athletes.

Beth finished her run and returned to the dorm to enjoy a hot shower. She didn't bother drying her hair, she simply brushed it out and put it in a ponytail. She quickly put on a pair of jeans, a T-shirt, sneakers, and one of her many sweatshirts and headed out by herself to the cafeteria.

When she got there, she sat with a few of the freshman girls she knew from her hall in the dorm. She enjoyed their company and they seemed to admire her humor and outgoingness, but she still wasn't particularly close to any of them. Beth finished a rather unexciting meal, said her goodbyes, and returned to her room to study for Monday's "Forest Biometrics" test. She was currently majoring in Forestry. She knew she loved everything about being outdoors, especially being in the woods, but she wasn't completely committed to her major. In high school, she wasn't sure what she wanted to do and had little help from overloaded school counselors. She finally decided she would get most of her required classes out of the way, giving her more time to determine the best career path. She was passionate about athletics but wasn't convinced there was a strong job market in the related fields. She was still considering health and physical education, sports management, or sports medicine. She knew she would need to make the decision before the next semester started. She felt a little anxious about this because her finances were limited, and she couldn't afford to waste any of it on additional classes. Beth's funding for college came from a combination of academic scholarships, Lacrosse scholarships, state aid, and her own savings. She had no financial support from any family members. Beth tragically lost her parents when she was thirteen. They were hit and killed by a drunk driver. Beth only had one much older brother, David, with whom she lived after their death. Beth still fondly remembered her mother's answer to why there was such an age difference between her and David, "You were a very special surprise gift. The best gift God could ever give me." This thought helped her when she fought through depression and wanted to give up.

After an hour of studying, Beth put down her book and notes and slid her chair away from her desk. She pulled her arms back behind her head and stretched out her stiff muscles. Her tight biceps popped out of her dark arms as she let out a loud sigh. She stepped on the heels of her running shoes so that she wouldn't have to untie them and pulled them halfway off. She then took aim at the large green trash can across the room and flicked a sneaker at it. She missed. "Basket", she said quietly as the second landed on top of crumpled paper in the trash can. Then she turned on the T.V. and laid back to watch her favorite Sunday night news show, "*60 Minutes*". Her thoughts drifted back to running. She decided that tomorrow she would run the same route and go around the same time as she did today.

Perhaps, she thought, she might run into the young woman she had passed today.

CHAPTER TWO

Meeting Anne

As the sun peeked through the window and began to shine upon her face, Beth began to move. Suddenly she sat straight up. She tried to gain a sense of time, noticing that the TV was still on. Quickly she realized that it was morning and she had slept straight through the night. She panicked. She only had ten minutes to get to class to take the test. There was no time to change and freshen up, so she ran to the bathroom, combed her hair, and brushed her teeth. She grabbed her jacket, flipped off the TV and anxiously hurried out, letting the door slam behind her.

As she ran along the walk heading to class, she managed to relax enough to wonder if Chris was all right. She had never stayed out all night with her boyfriend before. What if something bad had happened to her? How much time should she wait before she called the police? She was making herself nervous thinking about all the things that could have happened. She realized that she and Chris should talk this over the next time they saw each other.

Soon Beth was at the doors of a huge ivy-covered building. She pushed the door open and held it for the girl who had just run up behind her. "Thank you," a voice said politely.

"You're welcome," Beth replied. Suddenly she realized it was the runner she had passed the other day. The young woman recognized her.

"Boy…you must really like to run! I watched you sprint halfway across campus."

Beth laughed nervously. She knew her face was red. "Actually, I overslept. I'm late for a test."

"Ahhh…sounds like too much running and too little sleep," the young woman warned sweetly as they started to climb the steps to their classrooms.

"No, no…I wish that were it!" They reached the second floor and the young woman started heading off towards her destination. Suddenly, she stopped and asked, "Hey, do you want to run together sometime?"

"Yeah, I guess so." Beth said, trying to hide her excitement.

"Okay, great! We don't have time to exchange numbers now so I'll just see you around, then we can decide when. Oh, by the way, what's your name?"

Feeling somewhat stupid, even as she was saying it, she replied "Beth Locke, with an 'E' at the end."

The young woman laughed a little and responded, "Well I'm Anne Stetson with an 'E' at the end of Anne."

Beth smiled shyly and laughed as she turned and raced to the third floor, taking two steps at a time. She couldn't believe she was still blushing. It was unlike her to be shy around anyone. It wasn't a bad feeling; it was simply different. She realized that she was more excited about running with Anne, than about anything else that had happened since she started school.

Beth glanced at her watch as she entered the classroom. She was ten minutes late. She walked across the front of the room and sat down in a chair. She could feel herself trying not to grin, she was still so excited. A balding, short, and stocky professor came by her desk and laid a multiple page test on it. "You're a little late dear."

"Yes, I'm sorry about that," she responded feeling like she was the center of attention, but not really caring if she was. The professor stared at her for a moment and then said, "Please don't let it happen again."

"No sir...I won't," she nodded. She started her exam by just looking over the questions. They seemed to cover the information that she had studied, but she became a little nervous that the questions might become more difficult towards the end. She had always been a high honors student, but this was college, so she didn't know what to expect. Having good grades was one of Beth's many self-imposed expectations. She had always worked harder than most to achieve any goal she set. Would this be enough to succeed in college?

CHAPTER THREE

A Rabbit and A Deer

Only a few days had passed before Beth saw Anne again, but it felt much longer. Anne was almost always on Beth's mind. She was both eager and nervous about the run. Beth wasn't sure she was fast enough to keep up with Anne and wouldn't want to hold her back. She knew she would be embarrassed if that happened and was convinced that Anne would never want to run with her again.

It was Friday afternoon, and Beth was on her way to join a long line of impatient students waiting to pick up their permanent college I.D. cards. As she approached, she heard someone yell, "Hey Beth, come up here." It was Anne, standing with a group of people. She had let her blonde hair down and was wearing an expensive looking sweater and jeans. Anne looked like the perfect All-American girl. By anyone's standard, she was eye-catching. Beth imagined that some people might be jealous of Anne's looks, making unfair judgements about her. Still, Beth found herself trying not to be intimidated by Anne's beauty as she walked towards her. Anne introduced Beth to her friends as a "fellow runner" then moved closer for a more private conversation.

"Boy, I thought I'd never see you again. You must have been hiding," Anne said smiling.

"No, no. I've been around, but I guess we just didn't cross paths." She was sure of that because she had been diligently watching for her.

"Well, do you still want to run with me?"

"Sure, just tell me when," Beth said, still feeling a little unsure of herself.

"How about this afternoon at three o'clock?"

"All right, where should I meet you?"

Anne thought for a second and then asked, "What dorm are you in?"

"Brownstone."

"Okay, I'll meet you in the lobby at three o'clock. That'll give you an hour. I'm really looking forward to this Beth," Anne said smiling.

Beth could not control a grin, "Me too."

It was five of three when Beth entered the Brownstone lobby. She was dressed in only shorts, and a lacrosse T-shirt. With the autumn air, she knew she might feel a little cold when she started her run, but it wouldn't be long before she was sweating. As she waited, she started to feel nervous. She worried about keeping pace with Anne, and she worried about carrying on interesting conversations as they ran. Then she realized that the pace may be so fast, that talking to each other might not even be an option.

At three o'clock sharp, Anne pushed her way through the swinging glass doors. She looked even taller in her tight running shorts, and a sports top that revealed her slim athletic body.

"Ready?" she asked with bright eyes and a big grin.

"I think so," Beth said with a hint of sarcasm. "Where do you want to run?"

"Well...how about the cross-country course?"

"Okay, I just hope I can keep up with you," Beth added modestly as she checked the lacing on her sneakers to hide the fact that she was blushing. Anne just shook her head and smiled as they headed out the door.

Little talking took place while they ran. They were saving their energy for those endless hills. They kept an

21

even pace. It was a fast one and Beth was pushing to keep it. Between breaths, Anne let out, "Do you always run this course at this pace?"

"No!" Beth almost yelled, then she paused to catch a few mouthfuls of air, "I'm just following you."

"Me?" Anne yelled, "I've been following YOU!" Beth let out a little laugh and managed to say, "Well we've kept the pace this far, let's see if we can keep it going."

"All right," Anne agreed, "As long as you're strong enough to carry me home!"

The remainder of the run was silent. It had to be. They couldn't waste any more energy.

Just as they approached the final stretch, they looked at each other, smiled, and without further communications, began sprinting towards the finish line. They crossed the line shoulder to shoulder, not a step in front or behind one another. They slowed their pace to an easy jog in order to catch their breath and cool down their bodies.

Their faces were covered with sweat and their wet shirts revealed how hard they had worked.

"I never thought I'd make it," Anne admitted still breathing heavily.

"Me neither!"

Anne gave Beth a supportive pat on the back. "Well, we did it!" she beamed proudly. Beth looked over into Anne's eyes and held her gaze. She gave her the smile she could no longer hold back.

As soon as they were cooled down enough to walk, Anne said teasingly, "I probably wouldn't have made it, if you weren't so effortlessly cruising along next to me making me feel guilty about wanting to slow down."

Beth was quick to reply to the compliment, "It certainly wasn't effortless. I was pushing just as hard, if not harder than you. I've never run that fast, for that long before."

"I guess we just bring out the best in each other." Anne said and grinned playfully, staring directly into Beth's eyes. Beth laughed, not knowing what to say. It made her feel wonderfully uncomfortable.

"I think we'd make a good team Beth," then added with a more serious tone, "I really do…"

"I guess we'll just have to find out when we run again." Beth replied with an impish smile.

As they went through their cool down stretching routines, Anne asked Beth a few general questions, like how old she was, what her major was, and what other sports she played. Beth returned the questions and learned that Anne lived off campus in an apartment she shared with two other girls, and that she was a twenty-year-old Junior taking pre-med classes. She also discovered that Anne had played tennis her freshman and sophomore years but stopped to concentrate more on her studies. She said that running track didn't consume as much time, and she planned to run again this year and her senior year. She kiddingly asserted she was a "proud miler" because she believed it was the most demanding event and she liked a challenge. Beth enjoyed listening to Anne, and the more information Anne offered, the more Beth's admiration for her grew.

As they walked towards the campus, Anne confided, "I really enjoyed this." Then she looked down at her sweaty body and kidded, "I think!"

Beth's grin showed her agreement, then surprising herself, she asked eagerly "Do you want to run tomorrow?"

"Oh…I can't this weekend."

Beth felt a twinge of disappointment, but Anne added quickly and enthusiastically, "How about Monday? Same time?"

Beth nodded, "Okay, Monday's fine."

"Good! Maybe if I run with you more often, I might get in shape. You're really fast Beth," she declared sincerely.

Beth's face reddened with the praise, she shook her head and began to say "No I'm not…" but Anne quickly interrupted, "Ahhh…you must be one of those modest athletes, my favorite type. I'm not a big fan of big egos."

"I'm not being modest I'm just convinced I'm not as fast as you."

"Now how do you know that? We just met and we've only run once together."

"Well, just look at your build!" Beth pointed with her hands as she talked. "You're thin, tall, strong and you run like a deer."

"Well, have you looked at yourself? You're nothing but lean muscle, and you run like a rabbit." They looked at each other and laughed at the same time.

"I'll tell you what," Anne said, "on Monday we'll race on the cross-country course."

"No! I don't want to race you. I'll make a fool of myself!"

"No, you won't, besides it's good training. It will help us get ready for track season."

"How do you know if I'm going out for track? I don't even know if I want to!"

"You better!" Anne smiled warmly, "We can't have raw talent like yours go to waste."

Beth enjoyed the flattery but didn't want to show it. "How about we talk about it on Monday?" she conceded as they reached her dorm.

"Sure, that's fine with me. I'll see you then." Beth had the urge to hug Anne goodbye, like she did with a lot of her friends, but she couldn't find the courage to do it. She just smiled, "I'll see you, thanks for the run," then watched Anne take off, jogging across the college's grass courtyard. Monday couldn't come fast enough.

CHAPTER FOUR

"Kiss on the Cheek"

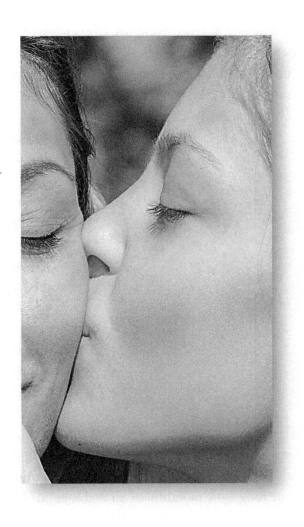

Beth went with her roommate to the cafeteria for dinner that evening. She was eager to tell Chris about meeting and running with Anne, but Chris seemed disinterested, so Beth kept her excitement to herself. Having dinner together did provide them the opportunity however, to establish some guidelines for communicating with each other if they weren't going to be coming back to the dorm for the night. This would be one of those evenings. Chris's boyfriend picked her up later that night. Beth had the room to herself but had no reason to take advantage of it. She just wanted to watch some TV and go to bed early, so she could get up at six o'clock and run.

On Saturday morning, Beth ran down to the cross-country course. The air was brisk, but warm enough to wear just a pair of black running shorts, white T-shirt and baseball hat. She stretched her stiff muscles, then positioned herself at the starting line. She inhaled one long slow mouthful of air and took off bursting with fresh energy. She ran through the woods, leaping over logs and dodging rocks and branches along the path. She ran hard, working her mind as well as her body. She took note of which parts of the course she could safely pick up her pace, and where she had to ease up. She plotted the descents that would provide her body time to recover. She wanted to become familiar with the course so that she could plan to run it for speed. She finished the course exhausted but satisfied.

After lunch on Saturday, Beth ran the course again. Then once again on Sunday morning, but not quite as hard, because she wanted to save her legs. As she ran, she could only think about Anne, and what it would be like to get to see her again. She didn't care as much about winning as she thought she would. She was more anxious about disappointing her new friend.

Monday morning went much too slowly for Beth. Classes seemed to last forever. Three o'clock just couldn't come quick enough. She was ready twenty minutes early and waited eagerly in the lobby. Anne was right on time.

"Hi Anne," Beth said as soon as she saw her.

"Hey girl…" she responded as if they had been friends for a long time. "Did you have a nice weekend?"

"Yeah…I guess, but they're always too short." She didn't want to admit it felt much too long. "How about you?"

"I spent most of the time studying and just hanging out with friends." Beth imagined that Anne would have a lot of good friends.

"Well let's get going!" she said as she playfully grabbed Beth by the arm and guided her to the door. Beth enjoyed Anne's touch.

They went outside and began warming up on the grass. Beth wore a sweatshirt, and Anne had a jacket. They had to be extra careful today because it was colder than it had been. Even though their muscles were still tight, both seemed as flexible as gymnasts. While they were sitting on the ground stretching, a young woman snuck up behind Anne and put her hands on her shoulders and gave a squeeze. Anne looked back,

"Hey Carol! How are you?" Carol was a little taller than Beth and had fair skin and red hair. Beth thought she was very attractive, and based on her build, assumed she was an athlete.

"I'm fine," Carol said. "I didn't see you around this weekend. Where were you hiding?"

"I was holed up in my apartment studying." Beth noticed that Anne left out the part about hanging out with other people.

"I want you to meet a friend of mine. This is Beth. She'll be running track with us this year." Beth just nodded and said "Hi". She was pleased that Anne introduced her as her "friend".

"You look like you're getting ready to run. If you could wait a half hour, I could join you." Beth felt an immediate sense of disappointment. She had been looking forward to time alone with Anne and didn't want to share it.

"Carol, I am so sorry…it would be great to run together but I have an obligation that I'm going to have trouble keeping as it is. Can we get a rain check?" Beth sensed that Carol was hoping for a different answer.

"All right, but don't forget to call me and we can set something up."

"Sounds good, I will." They said their goodbyes and Carol headed into Brownstone, Beth's dorm.

Beth was curious about the obligation Anne had, but was happy that Carol was not joining them. It would have changed everything. Anne looked over at Beth and asked if she was loose enough to start running. She never offered her any more information about Carol or what obligation she had, so Beth didn't ask.

"Okay...let's run down to the course slowly, so we can get our blood flowing."

"Are we still going to race?" Beth had to know.

Anne started jogging, "We won't call it a race. Let's just say we will run our best."

When they reached the starting area, Beth pulled off her sweatshirt and laid it on the ground. Anne did the same with her jacket, taking a stopwatch out of the pocket.

"Ready?" Anne asked, as she set the timer. Beth moved up next to her on the starting line and shook her head no. "I love competition, but not against my own teammates and friends." Anne grinned, "Too bad... GO!"

Beth began her run a little faster than she ran over the weekend. She wasn't sure she could keep up, but she would give it every effort she could muster. Anne stayed by her side. Halfway through, Beth said, breathing heavily, "You don't have to stay with me...you can run ahead."

"I wish I could!" Anne quickly replied.

When they neared the end, Beth gave her final kick. Anne stayed right beside her. Once again, they finished side by side. Anne pushed the button on the stopwatch and tried to slow down enough to read it. Beth felt nauseated. She slowed down but couldn't quite stop yet. She felt like she might throw up. She needed to cool down. Finally, Beth bent over still trying to catch her breath.

"This is great!" Anne said as she joined Beth.

"I don't feel so great…" Beth groaned.

Anne handed her the stopwatch. Beth was clueless, "Is this a good time for the course?"

"Yes! It's almost as good as the cross-country team's top runners."

"Maybe we're missing our calling." Beth said half-jokingly.

"Nope, I'm a miler through and through, and I want you to be too. I really believe we'd make a good team. We seem to motivate each other. We must have some type of special connection," Anne said grinning. Beth gave a little laugh but was truly thrilled and surprised that Anne said that. She loved the idea that they might have a "special connection."

Anne flopped down on the grass and laid on her back. Beth decided she would do the same and placed herself only a couple feet away. Beth was very conscious of Anne's body next to her. She could feel her warmth and hear her breathing. Neither spoke for a moment until Beth nervously broke the silence. "So…when do we start training?"

"I'm ready when you are. I live off campus so when we get back to your dorm, I'll write down my number and you can give me a call and tell me what works for you?"

"Wow...you're going to give me your number? I do feel special now." Although Beth said it as a joke, she panicked and thought, why the hell did I say that? She's going to think I'm weird!

Anne smirked, "I already told you I thought you were special. I don't give many people my number, so don't lose it," she kidded.

Beth waited a day before she called, not wanting to look too eager. She had taped the paper with Anne's number on it, to the shelf above her desk. She took it down a couple of times and studied Anne's handwriting. It was very neat, just as Beth expected. She smiled to herself at the thought that Anne's beautiful handwriting might change once she becomes a doctor.

Beth started to call Anne several times that evening but hung up before it rang. She wasn't sure exactly what she wanted to say. Finally, she made the call and arrangements were made to run the following day.

When Beth woke the next morning, it was dark and drizzling. Throughout her morning classes Beth watched the sky hoping that it would clear up by afternoon. By two forty-five though, the sky had only grown cloudier and the rain was coming down harder. With disappointment, she called Anne to confirm the cancellation, but no one answered. She figured Anne had probably gone out somewhere for the afternoon. She changed out of her school clothes and into a pair of shorts, and T-shirt. Then she threw on her favorite sweatshirt from her high school Lacrosse team.

Beth selected a textbook from the shelf and laid down on her bed to study. She was warm and comfy, but still disappointed that she wouldn't be able to run with Anne.

"Hey...I waited for a while down in the lobby." The voice startled Beth. She looked up and saw Anne's head peeking in the doorway.

"Oh shit...come in," she said genuinely surprised.

Anne entered the room and teased, "I got tired of waiting so I looked up your room number. What are you still doing up here? Pretending you're studying? You're not going to let this rain prevent us from running, are you?"

Beth jumped up from the bed, "No, no, I tried to call you. I didn't think you would want to run, but I'm dressed and ready."

"You don't know me well enough yet, but you'll find out that if I say something, I really mean it! You're my training partner now, so we're going to be seeing a lot of each other, no matter what the weather, or anything else that might try to get in our way."

They ran the mud-covered course with as much energy and determination as they had in the past two runs and finished just as exhausted. When they recovered, they started jogging back to Beth's dorm in their saturated, muddy clothing. Beth got the courage to invite Anne back up to her room. Anne accepted. When they reached her room, Beth offered her a dry T-shirt. Anne seemed to hesitate, but then said, "I can't stay too long, but I think I would feel a lot better with this off," pointing to her drenched T-shirt. Beth knew that Anne would need a dry pair of shorts too, so she grabbed a pair of her own assuming they would fit because of their similar builds.

Anne took the white tee shirt from Beth's hand and pulled off the saturated one.

"Can you help me with this?" Anne said as she put her back to Beth indicating she needed assistance in getting her wet bra up and over her head.

"Sure," Beth said as if it was no big deal, but her dark face was flushing a bright red. Anne's back was fully exposed. Beth was impressed by how strong it was. You could almost see the separation between each muscle. Her tan skin made the muscle definition look even more remarkable. Beth felt guilty admiring Anne's body, but couldn't help herself. She finished helping Anne pull the bra over her head then quickly said, "I'm going to get changed in the bathroom." She grabbed something to throw on and headed straight to the bathroom before Anne had a chance to turn around. Beth changed into a pair of warm sweats and a clean T-shirt. Anne was looking at some of the pictures on Beth's desk when Beth came out.

"Is this handsome man your boyfriend?" she inquired as she held up a picture.

"No way. That's my brother."

"You have to admit he is good looking."

"I won't be telling him that you said that, because it would go right to his head". Anne shared that she was a single child, and that she often wished she had brothers to play with and compete against. She thought it would have made her a better athlete.

"It probably would have, but you're already a star," Beth teased. Beth never shared any more information about her family.

"Are you seeing anyone?" Anne asked.

Beth felt her face flush. "Not right now. My boyfriend and I decided to part ways when we went to different colleges in different states." It was mostly true. "How about you?"

"No, not right now," Anne said very matter-of-factly. "But my roommates keep trying to set me up." Beth couldn't believe it. She imagined Anne having guys hanging all over her. She wanted to ask her why she didn't have a boyfriend, but instead said, "Good. Then we can focus on our training better with no distractions."

The subject was dropped, and they spent the next hour talking and laughing about a variety of topics. Most of their conversation was concerning track. Anne filled her in on some of the girls on the track team. She mentioned Carol as one of the other milers and credited Carol with having worked hard to turn her raw talent in to that of an experienced successful runner. She said they trained a lot together before, but she personally felt that Beth would be a better training partner. She wanted them all to go for a run together before the season started though. Beth wasn't thrilled with the idea.

Beth felt comfortable talking with Anne. Neither of them discussed anything intimately personal, but they were still getting to know each other. Anne told Beth more about her living arrangements. She said her two roommates already had the apartment since last year and were looking for someone to share the bills with. Michaela, who she met in a pre-med study group, asked her if she would be interested in joining them for this school year. "I wanted to get out of the dorms, so I didn't hesitate in saying yes," Anne said.

36

"That was good timing, wasn't it?" Beth said thinking she should at least add something to the conversation.

"I swear though Beth...they're exact opposites. Michaela is an absolutely beautiful African American woman who is very proper and sweet. You know, the kind that never curses. She's a ballet dancer here at school and she teaches dance during the summer. She and my other roommate, Liza, have been friends since they were assigned the same dorm room freshman year. Liza is an art major. She is second generation Japanese. Her real name is Leiko, but everyone calls her Liza because 'Leiko' in Japanese represents arrogance. Liza's grandmother tried to stop her mom from naming her that, but her mom insisted that it really should mean assertive. She said women who are called arrogant, are usually strong women who are just being confident and asserting themselves. That attribute describes Liza perfectly."

"Do you all get along?" Beth asked.

"Yes, we haven't had any problems so far, even though we're all very different. We actually are so busy that we don't see each other that much during the week. Liza and Michaela do a lot of things together though, especially on weekends. They'll go and stay at each other's homes sometimes."

"How about chores?" Beth asked.

"We share the chores, which is no big deal because we're all clean freaks. We did agree however, that we wouldn't let any boyfriends stay over, and so far, that hasn't been a problem. Liza has a lot of guy friends, but I think only one of them is her boyfriend. Occasionally she doesn't come home, but she always calls. Michaela has a steady boyfriend, but I don't know if they're even having sex yet." Beth just laughed and kidded, "What about you? Has that 'no boyfriends staying over' rule, make you change your lifestyle?"

"Nope…not at all," Anne said smiling.

They continued to talk for another hour. They shared personal thoughts and feelings such as who they admired, some of their favorite memories, the things they loved to do and the things they hated to do. Anne was a good listener. She made Beth feel like whatever she had to say was either important or interesting. Beth loved Anne's keen sense of humor and quick wit. Whenever she was in Anne's company, Beth seemed to be either smiling or laughing.

When Anne stood to leave, she said with a devilish grin, "I'm going to push us even harder tomorrow, you better be ready!" Then she gave Beth a hug goodbye with a kiss on her cheek. Beth's own family and friends gave hugs and kisses when they met or parted, and she never thought twice about it. This time however, it felt different. This time, she was very aware of that kiss.

CHAPTER FIVE

Carol

Beth settled into a daily routine of breakfast, consisting of peanut butter toast and fruit, attending two classes, lunch, one or two more classes, and then meeting up with Anne to train. After their run, she would head back to the dorm to shower, have dinner and then study. She found she was a little distracted while studying because she kept thinking about Anne. Still, she managed to maintain good grades and was beginning to enjoy college life.

After two weeks of running, mostly on the cross-country course, they started to do workouts on the track. Beth proved herself to be equally competent on the surface of the track as she was on the compacted dirt and gravel.

A close friendship was developing quickly, almost as rapidly as their running times were dropping. They kidded and teased each other frequently but shared a few of their more serious thoughts and ideas too. Beth's fondness of Anne grew. She noticed and liked the way Anne walked, her voice, her laughter, even the way she brushed back her long blond hair. She felt a sense of pride to be considered Anne's "good friend". She realized that she was developing a typical crush, except this time it was on another girl. She wondered if anyone in high school had ever felt this way about her. There were a couple of girls that might have, but it didn't bother her. She enjoyed their attention. She was certain however she should never let Anne know how she felt because it might ruin their friendship.

After a few weeks of training, Beth got a call from Anne, asking if it would be okay for Carol to join them on the cross-country course. She explained that Carol had called and suggested they run together.

"I told her that I train with you, but I didn't think you would mind if she joined us. Is that okay?"

"Of course, that's fine," she proclaimed, but wasn't really feeling the sincerity of her answer.

"All right then, she's going to meet us there. She offered me a ride, but I told her I was going to meet you in the lobby as usual."

"Do you think she can keep up with us?" Beth asked with a forced smile.

"I spent a lot of time with her, so I know how good she is. If she's training as hard as we have, there's a good chance that she will. Maybe the three of us could cross the finish line at the same time."

"Well…I guess we'll just have to wait and see." Beth grinned as she said it, but what she was thinking was, "No freaking way…"

Beth and Anne met Carol at the beginning of the course. Beth watched Anne give Carol a hug and kiss on the cheek, just as she did with her. They made some small talk about the weather and the condition of the course. It rained the night before, so the course was going to be muddy and slippery. As soon as they agreed they were stretched and ready, they lined up, side by side. Beth noticed that Anne did not have her stopwatch this time.

They took off with Anne and Carol in front, because only two people could fit across the narrow path at the start of the course. When the path widened, they all ran next to each other. The pace was fast, but not so fast that they couldn't talk. Most of their words were warnings about dangerous spots on the course. Beth noticed that Anne supported Carol by the elbow a couple of times, particularly in slippery areas. She also noted that Carol reciprocated the gesture. They continued to keep the same pace. It was not a pace that would win any prizes, but it still challenged their cardio. As they got closer to the end, Beth wondered if she and Anne would finish as they always did, side by side in an all-out sprint. They soon hit their mark and Beth started her sprint. It seemed the other two were doing the same thing, until Carol hit a slippery spot and her feet went out from under her. She landed hard on her back in a pool of mud. Anne stopped immediately and attended to Carol.

"Oh my God, are you okay?" she said in a panicked voice. "Are you okay to get up?"

"Oh shit…I can't believe I did that!" Carol said with a combination of humor and embarrassment.

"Here, let me help you up," Anne said as she reached out and took Carol's hands to pull her up.

As soon as Beth realized what happened, she turned around and jogged back to them. She saw how sincerely concerned Anne was, as she put her arm around Carol's waist to support her. Carol put her arm around Anne's shoulder as they walked. Beth offered to help, but they said they were okay, so she just walked behind them. She saw that Carol's butt was covered in mud and found it a little funny. She immediately admonished herself for thinking that. She realized this apparent accident could have been serious. She wasn't sure how much pain Carol was in, but she seemed to be walking fine. She still hadn't taken her arm off Anne's shoulder, and Anne still had her arm securely around Carol's waist. Beth felt out of the picture. She couldn't see being of much help anyway.

They held on to each other until Anne helped Carol back to the car. Carol swore she was fine and would probably only have a few embarrassing bruises. Beth caught herself thinking that Carol might not be hurt at all. Whatever the truth was, she was getting Anne's full attention and sympathy. Before Carol got into the car, Anne grabbed a towel from the back, and put it on the driver's seat. She gave her a gentle hug and a soft kiss on the lips, "Promise you'll give me a call tonight or I'm coming over to check on you!"

"Don't worry...I'm fine."

"Okay...I love you. Be careful driving home."

Beth was ashamed of herself for thinking Carol might not call Anne, just so Anne would have to come over. She also noted that Anne had never said, "Love you" to her, when they parted. Carol got in her car and took off. Anne started walking with Beth back to the dorm.

"Wow...can you believe that? I hope she's okay," Anne said sincerely.

"Me too. She really took a fall. I'm glad you were there to help her. I would have helped but I didn't realize what had happened at first."

"Oh God...don't feel guilty about that! I know you would have helped." Beth wasn't quite sure she did feel any guilt.

"It was my job to take care of her anyway. Carol and I have been very good friends for a while. I guess you could say, we knew each other quite well in high school." Her tone of voice and the way she looked at Beth made her think that Anne was going to admit something important. Anne's blatant honesty sometimes made Beth nervous.

"Carol ended up going to a different college on a track scholarship. I think she was hurt that we weren't going to be attending the same one. But I was okay with it. I needed a little space. Carol kind of attached herself to me. She told me that she had a crush on me when I was a senior and she was a junior. I guess I was just flattered by her interest in me, so we got together for a short time."

"What do you mean 'got together'? Were you running partners?" Beth asked naively.

"No...you know, we kind of fooled around sometimes," Anne laughed nervously, seeming surprised that Beth didn't know what she meant. Beth was beginning to understand exactly what Anne was implying. She couldn't believe what she was hearing. She was shocked that Anne had the guts to admit it.

"Oh..." was the only thing Beth could squeak out. Her mind was flooded with different images, she only imagined Anne with good looking guys. She knew she had dated boys because she had shared stories about some of her dates. Anxious questions filled Beth's mind. Does she know how I feel about her? Does she see me like Carol and think I might get too attached? Do I actually want to "fool around" too? What the hell is happening here? She felt emotionally overwhelmed.

"Does that bother you?" Anne asked earnestly.

"No, not at all." She wasn't sure what she felt but thought that was the answer Anne wanted to hear.

"I hope that won't change our friendship," Anne said, as though she was genuinely concerned.

"Of course not. We're just friends, I don't care what your past involves. It's nobody's business but yours."

"Good. Then we agree. Now let's head back."

Beth thought Anne was acting as though this was no big deal, but judging by Anne's flushed face, Beth sensed that for the first time, Anne might be a little embarrassed. Beth had a lot more questions but felt she shouldn't ask them. Suddenly though, like getting a slap on the back of the head, a new realization hit her, and she blurted out, "I thought you said Carol went to another college?"

"She did, but she transferred here this year".

"Oh..." was all Beth said quietly.

CHAPTER SIX

Marshmallows for Two

Beth could think of nothing else for the next couple of days. She and Anne never spoke of the conversation again, as if they had made an unspoken agreement.

It was Friday and Carol hadn't joined them since the cross-country run. They had planned their work out specifically for the track, and it would be the hardest they had to push all week. At times they felt like they weren't going to make it, but they motivated each other with a sympathetic look, and encouraging words. After they completed their cool down, Anne, obviously exhausted, laid back on the grass as she often did. Beth wasn't sure if she should do the same this time, because of their conversation about Carol. She laid down anyway, convincing herself that the cool grass would feel good on her sweaty body. She plopped down with a loud sigh and ended up closer to Anne than she intended. So close in fact that when Anne turned to talk to her, their bodies almost touched. Beth felt a familiar warm flush fill her. She didn't mean to violate Anne's personal space, but she chose not to back away.

"We should celebrate tonight!" Anne said enthusiastically as she raised up on her elbow. "I think we deserve it. Do you drink or are you a dedicated athlete?"

Beth, still aware of Anne's closeness, thought it might feel strange if she turned towards her. If she did, she would be intimately close to Anne's face and staring directly into her eyes. The image was undeniably inviting. She could feel her heartbeat starting to race. She wanted to turn towards her, but she didn't. She just kept looking straight up into the slowly darkening sky.

"Although I am a dedicated athlete," she joked, "I think we should celebrate. I'm not a big drinker though." It was true. Beth didn't drink much in high school. She had never been drunk, and was proud of that, especially after watching others make fools of themselves.

"Okay then...I've got a good idea about how we can celebrate! I'll surprise you," Anne said eagerly.

"Oh no... I'm not so sure I should have agreed," she whispered just loud enough for Anne to hear.

"Oh, don't worry...we'll have a lot of fun." Anne said with a big grin.

Anne laid back down and they rested quietly in the grass, catching glimpses of the sun set through the trees. After a few minutes of silence, Anne asked, "Are you ready to go back?"

Beth wanted to say no, but she forced out the words, "I guess so."

Anne stood up quickly and stretched out her hands to pull Beth up. Beth reached up and wrapped her fingers around Anne's hands and held on firmly. A delightful feeling raced through her body. She pulled herself up slowly and thanked Anne for the help.

Anne shared her plan for the first part of the evening, "Okay, I'll go home and shower, then I'll come back and pick you up. I'll need about an hour. I'll meet you in front of the dorm."

"Sounds good. I desperately need a shower. I must smell bad...I sweated like a pig today," Beth joked as she pretended to smell her shirt.

Beth waited for Anne outside of her dorm. Soon Anne drove up in a black BMW convertible. "Where did you steal this?" Beth kidded.

"It was my Dad's. He handed it down to me when his company gave him a new one. He said I'll have to pay it off after I graduate and get a job, and believe me, he means it." The inside of the car was as Beth expected, exceptionally clean and it smelled brand new.

Anne drove to an apartment building to pick up her friends, Mia, and Abby, who were waiting outside. Mia was a twenty-one-year-old senior, and Abby was a junior. They both ran the 400-meter relay on the track team. Anne told Beth it would just be the four of them.

She shared that Carol had called earlier and asked her if she would come over to her apartment, just to hang out. Anne told Carol how much she genuinely appreciated the offer, but explained that she already had plans, and they would find another time to get together. Beth wanted to ask if she told Carol that she was one of the people that Anne planned to be with. She decided to keep that thought to herself.

The four girls headed to the closest liquor store, all squeezed comfortably into Anne's small convertible with the top down.

"It's my turn to pay!" Anne had to yell to Mia in the back seat because the wind made it so noisy. Then Anne explained to Beth, who sat next to her, that Mia would be the one to go into the store to buy the liquor, because she was the only one old enough. It clearly sounded to Beth like this was not their first time doing this. Beth tried to insist on paying, but Anne just blew her off. Mia came out of the store with an abundant supply of beer and a bag full of snacks.

"Did you get any marshmallows?" Anne yelled out before Mia got into the car.

"Of course! You can't have a campfire without marshmallows."

At first, Beth found herself a bit uncomfortable amongst this group of upper classmen but was enjoying herself just the same. She heard two cans of beer being opened in the back seat as soon as they started driving. Anne described their destination as a popular "partying place". The location was in the woods behind the football field, close to the cross-country course.

By the time they reached a small dirt road leading into the woods, they were laughing loudly and carrying on. Beth was relaxed now and enjoying being a part of this adventure. They parked the car along the side of the road and headed down a small dark path. Anne was leading the way with a flashlight. Beth walked by her side, occasionally bumping shoulders because of the narrowness of the path. Within five minutes they reached a small clearing.

"We've made it!" Mia shouted. Anne placed her hand on Beth's shoulder, leaned towards her, and quietly and reassuringly said, "It will feel more comfortable once we get a fire going."

"I guess I better have a beer then," Beth said as she opened one up and took a swig. She found she wasn't particularly fond of the taste but felt obligated to drink, because they had put out the money.

It wasn't long before a fire was burning bright. Abby, Mia, and Anne provided most of the entertainment. Beth laughed so hard at their antics and stories that her stomach hurt. The four of them sat around the warm fire enjoying a perfect evening. Beth was happy. When Abby and Mia were sharing their stories, Beth was trying to catch glimpses of Anne, who sat across from her, in the light from the flames. She believed Anne would make the perfect model. She was tall, blond, blue eyed, with a perfect fit body, and in her opinion, more striking than any model she had ever seen. Beth was still daydreaming when she put a marshmallow on her stick and put it over the flames. Hell…she is absolutely gorgeous, Beth thought to herself, almost letting a smile out. Soon after Mia and Abby said they were going into the woods to pee, Beth realized her marshmallow was on fire. "Oh crap," Beth said loudly as she tried to put it out.

"You better start fresh," Anne said to Beth as she sat down next to her on the log. She was so close they were touching shoulders. Beth was caught off guard and a little nervous. Anne reached into the marshmallow bag and pulled out two.

"Here…put two on that. One for me and one for you." Beth carefully slid them down and tried to make sure she had enough room between them, so they didn't stick together.

"They can touch each other you know. No harm in getting close," Anne teased as she bumped Beth's shoulder with hers and looked into Beth's eyes. Beth felt her face flush. Anne didn't take her eyes off of her, "You know you remind me of a toasted marshmallow…you're a little crispy on the outside, but you're nothing but sweet softness on the inside."

"Is that supposed to be a compliment?" Beth asked laughing, trying to disguise her excitement about Anne's comment.

"Of course," Anne said with a big smile, then gave Beth a kiss on the cheek as she stood to go back to where she came from.

"Thanks… I think," Beth said. She knew she was blushing but hoping Anne couldn't see it because it was too dark. Beth liked Anne's attention. It almost felt like she was flirting with her. Her heart fluttered. "I feel like I'm in the mountains camping," Beth said, directing her comment to Anne. Then she quickly asked, "Do you ever go camping?"

"Only when I was in the girl scouts."

"That's not camping! Do you want to go with me sometime?" As an effect of the beer, Beth was talking louder and being socially bolder.

"All right! I'd love to go!" Anne responded with apparent eagerness. Beth was surprised. She hadn't imagined Anne would take her seriously, and it seemed that Anne was excited about the invitation. For some reason she always assumed that Anne would have better things to do. Beth began to give a detailed description of what they would see, where they would go, and what challenges they would take on. She was determined to take Anne rock climbing and rappelling,

"This could be very dangerous, unless you were instructed by someone who knows what they are doing, someone like me," Beth bragged. She explained that she owned all the equipment they needed. Beth always got excited when she spoke about camping. It was something she enjoyed almost as much as running. Suddenly she realized she might have sounded conceited, or even childish, so she finished by saying, "But you really don't want to hear about this. I must be boring you to death."

"No, no, go on. It's just that I've never seen you so excited or heard you talk so much," Anne said smiling warmly. Beth's cheeks began to redden, and she could feel the heat in them from her embarrassment.

Beth looked down at her empty beer can and somewhat timidly admitted, "It has to be the beer. It must make me talk too much."

"Well, I like that, so drink up," Anne said as she handed an unopened can to her. Beth realized that Anne was still on her first beer, while she was about to open her fourth. It really didn't surprise her that Anne, who was going to be driving, was acting so responsibly. That was just another thing she admired about Anne.

It must have been an hour that Beth sat drinking and being amused by her new friends. Throughout the night, Beth, who was sitting across the fire from Anne, would watch Anne, even when Anne wasn't talking. One time however, when Beth looked up from fidgeting with a stick, she found Anne's eyes focused on her. Anne looked away and said nothing, but Beth sensed that Anne knew she had been caught. Beth held her gaze though, hoping Anne would glance back, but it didn't happen. A minute later though, Anne suddenly directed, "Come on Beth. Let's show these girls what track is all about."

"Whatever you say coach," Beth teased.

"All right you two, set up our hurdles while we warm up," she yelled to Mia and Abby as she pointed to some logs alongside the path. Anne was familiar with jumping hurdles. She competed in the hurdles when she was younger. The girls complied and created a small wall, no more than three feet high. Anne unzipped her windbreaker and pulled it off, then she pulled her bulky sweater over her head and kiddingly threw it at Beth.

"Now I'm ready."

Beth followed, taking off her hooded sweatshirt and announcing, "I'm ready too." Both girls amused themselves as they jogged around in their jeans and similar white tee shirts, trying to stay warm. It was obvious now, except for their height, how similar their builds were. They were lean, muscular, and womanly.

"You're taking too long," Anne yelled as she sprinted towards the makeshift hurdle, that was still in the process of being completed. Mia and Abby backed off as

Anne came flying over the logs. Her hurdle form was both graceful and well executed.

"Nothing to it," Anne yelled as she came running back. "Beth are you ready?"

"Not really... I've never run hurdles before, like you obviously have," she joked.

"Take a log off so it's lower," she told Mia and Abby. Then Abby encouraged Beth as she threw the log off to the side. "Just give it your best...think of it as an initiation onto the track team."

"If you insist," she offered "but don't laugh at me if I trip."

With that, Beth began running down the path, feeling a bit dizzy. She kept running though because she didn't want to disappoint Anne. When she felt she was close enough, she extended a straight leg over the logs, but her back leg caught, causing her to slam face first into the hard logs. You could hear the contact. Beth fell onto the ground. She laid on her back as she put both hands over her face.

"Oh my God!" Anne screamed and sprinted over to Beth.

"Oh, shit that hurt!" Beth joked loudly while keeping her hands over her face as if she was afraid of letting the others see what was beneath them.

"Just sit still. Let me see what's going on here," Anne said as she gently moved Beth's hands away from her face.

"You have a nice little cut, but you're going to be all right," she said calmly disguising the fact there was a large laceration over Beth's eyebrow that would need stitches. Blood started to drip into Beth's eyes and down her cheek. She kept trying to wipe it away with her hands.

"Someone go get a T-shirt out of the trunk," Anne demanded.

"I guess you wouldn't want me as a hurdler," Beth said flatly, trying to add some humor.

Abby rushed back with the T-shirt. Anne ripped it in half and put it around Beth's head to compress the wound. She used the other half to wipe some of the blood off Beth's face.

"How does your nose feel?" Anne asked with concern.

"No… it's fine. I just hit above my eye, and I already have a scar there anyway. The T-shirt was becoming saturated with blood. Anne put the other half of the torn shirt on top of it. Beth assumed Anne didn't want to pull the first one off because the blood was starting to clot, and that would just cause it to start bleeding heavily again.

"Mia, help me get her to the car. Abby go put out the fire." Anne directed without panic, but with certainty. The three of them carefully helped Beth to the car. Anne instructed them to put Beth in the back seat with her, and cautiously placed her head on her lap. Abby, who seemed quite sober, got in the driver's seat, and drove to the hospital. They were all quiet, except for Anne, who continued to talk to Beth to distract her from the pain, and to keep her awake. The second T-shirt strip was now saturated as well. Beth was going to need stitches, and there was a possibility that she had a concussion. Anne assured Beth that she would be all right but teased her that maybe she would end up with an even bigger looking scar, one that would make her look tougher. Beth tried to laugh.

Anne spoke sweetly as she stroked Beth's hair, in part to keep it away from the wound, and in part to soothe Beth. Beth was coherent enough to feel Anne's fingers playing with her hair, and she was very aware that her head was laying safely in Anne's lap.

Anne leaned forward and put her face close to Beth's. "Don't worry, we're almost there," she said softly. Beth could sense her warm breath. She didn't want to move, but she felt the need to show them she wasn't a "baby".

"I'm all right, I'm all right..." Beth insisted on trying to lift herself up from Anne's lap.

"Shhh... just keep still." Anne took Beth's hands and softly held them across Beth's chest, so she wouldn't try to get up.

"You know head wounds bleed a lot, so it's probably not as bad as you think," Beth said half kiddingly, trying to make everyone more relaxed, including herself.

"Oh my gosh Beth...will you just be quiet," Anne laughed.

"I'm sorry I ruined the party. I really am," she said seriously.

Anne was at a loss for words. She merely reached down and kissed Beth's forehead and said softly, "Oh Beth, you didn't. It was my fault, not yours. I'm so sorry I asked you to do something so stupid. I don't know what I was thinking."

Even through her pain, Beth could still feel her forehead tingle where Anne had just kissed her.

"I guess I don't know how to drink well."

"Shhh…we'll talk about this later."

The car pulled up to the emergency room entrance. They helped Beth out of the car while Mia went and got a wheelchair.

"I'm all right, I can walk," she complained politely, although she was feeling rather weak and dizzy. Anne held her and guided her into the wheelchair. The others walked beside her as Anne rolled her into the emergency room, and up to the receptionist's desk.

Anne placed her hands on Beth's shoulders and explained to the nurse that Beth had tripped and hit her face, which caused a deep cut above her eyebrow. Anne left out the other details. The nurse who looked to be in her sixties, skinny, with gray hair and glasses, appeared to be glaring at them. Anne suspected she knew alcohol was involved. Perhaps she could smell the beer that was most likely still on their breath.

"You college kids and your damn parties. It's a crying shame it takes a broken skull before you learn," she said crossly, without even looking up from her work. Beth was embarrassed and didn't know what to say. She turned and looked at Anne for help. Anne spoke up quickly but kept her voice low and calm.

"I would appreciate it greatly if you would save your anti-alcohol lectures for right now, and just get this young lady in to see a doctor," Anne stared into the nurse's eyes. Then added flatly, "Please."

The nurse stood up and headed for one of the small rooms down the corridor. As soon as the nurse was out of sight, they looked at each other and began to giggle. The look on the nurse's face was priceless. Beth was proud that Anne had the courage to stand up for her.

Anne told the others to go home and she would wait for Beth. Abby and Mia only had to make one call to find a friend to pick them up.

Anne waited patiently in the emergency room lobby, as the doctor carefully cleaned the wound, sewed it together with six stitches, and bandaged it in a sterile dressing. The doctor believed that Beth did not have a concussion but said she should still not be left alone overnight.

After an hour, Beth walked into the lobby with a white bandage over her eyebrow. Anne jumped up and smiled as she walked over to her. She waited for Beth to speak first as though she were waiting for a verdict.

"They said I'm good to go, and there is no concussion. They gave me a pill to ease the pain too."

"Thank God," Anne said as she took Beth's elbow and gently guided her out the hospital's big glass doors.

CHAPTER SEVEN

Pillow Talk

Anne drove Beth to her dorm and insisted that Beth wake up her roommate to watch over her, even though it was three o'clock in the morning. Beth didn't like the idea. She really didn't want Chris keeping her company, and she didn't want Anne to leave. She insisted that she would rather be alone than bother Chris. Anne walked her to her room just to make sure Beth got Chris up. When they went in, they discovered Chris's note explaining that she would not be back until Saturday afternoon.

"I'm staying," Anne said as if Beth didn't have a say in the decision. "I won't let you be here all by yourself."

"I feel fine, really!" Beth asserted. Anne didn't respond. She just gave her a look that implied Beth didn't stand a chance of changing her mind.

Beth smiled as she surrendered, "Okay. Then I'm not going to fight you. I don't think I would win anyway." Beth felt a little lightheaded, so she sat down on the edge of the bed.

Anne went over and pulled a washcloth off the towel rack, moistened it, then began to wipe some of the lingering blood off Beth's face and neck.

"I'm feeling maternal," Anne kidded sweetly. "Just let me take care of you." Beth looked down and blushed immediately.

"Good, I could use one," she said quietly. Anne stopped what she was doing. It seemed she recognized that Beth was uncomfortable. "I'm sorry, did I say something I shouldn't have?"

"No, no," Beth offered and smiled to relieve some of Anne's concern.

"It's just that my parents aren't living."

"Oh...I am so sorry Beth. I didn't know," Anne said, seeming embarrassed by her comment.

"That's okay." She laughed a little hoping to make Anne feel a little less awkward and embarrassed. "They died when I was thirteen. They were in a car accident. The driver of the other car and my parents were all killed. I'm okay talking about it now, but at the time it happened, I couldn't even think about it. It was a nightmare that I couldn't wake up from."

Beth felt comfortable sharing this heartbreaking story with Anne. She had only shared it with a few people. "I lived with my older brother David, who's ten years older than me and lived nearby. He had just gotten married. I lived with them until I came here to college."

"Do you have any younger brothers or sisters?" Anne asked.

"No, it was just me and David. I had a choice of living with this aunt, that I didn't know at all, or with my brother. I've really grown to appreciate him. If I were him, I don't think I would've taken me in, not with a new wife and all." Then she tried to add a little humor to the sadness, "But of course I was perfect." They both laughed. Beth continued, "No, I really did stay out of trouble. I would have felt horrible if I disappointed him. He gave up so much for me."

There was a stretch of silence until Anne spoke, "I'm so sorry Beth. I didn't mean to bring it up, especially after all that's happened this evening."

Beth sounded like she might be fighting off tears, "Oh, that's okay. Besides, I honestly believe that they're happy where they are now, and someday, we'll all be together again. I just miss them. I miss them every day."

Anne looked right into Beth eyes, as if she could feel Beth's grief.

Beth picked up on Anne's sympathy, "Please don't feel sorry for me! I really am okay now. I've grown to be happy again. You're one of the people that helped me get there." Beth couldn't believe she said that, but it was the absolute truth.

"Thank you, Beth...you make me happy too." Anne smiled at her then quietly said, "I think you need to get some rest. You must be exhausted." Beth was a little drowsy, but the news that she made Anne happy, made her feel wide awake. Now Beth wanted to talk. There was so much she needed to say but didn't have courage to say it. "Yeah, I guess you're right." Then she put her hand on Anne's shoulder, looked at her and said sincerely, "Thank you Anne. Thanks for taking care of me tonight...not that I needed it," she teased.

Anne smiled at her, "If it's okay with you, I'm going to stay here for what's left of the night." She didn't wait for an answer, she started to pull off her sneakers and unzip her pants.

"I guess I don't have much of a choice," Beth said smiling.

"You're right. You don't." Beth started to lay down, but Anne intervened,

"Aren't you going to change your clothes? You can't sleep in those blood-stained things!" Anne walked towards Beth as if she were going to help her take them off. Beth panicked for a second. She was still embarrassed to change in front of her, but realized that if she didn't do it herself, Anne was going to help her. She headed for her bureau, then pulled out a T-shirt and shorts, the ones she used as pajamas. She changed her shorts, then pulled the bloody shirt over her head, and slipped into the clean one without bothering to take off her bra. When she turned back around, Anne was folding her jeans and placing them over a chair. Beth hoped that Anne had been too busy to notice, but her hope was crushed when she heard Anne mumble, "Boy, you must be tired if you're leaving your bra on".

Beth had to make a quick decision. "Oh…you're right, I didn't even realize I had done that." Anne walked towards her saying, "Here let me unhook you." Beth thought she was going to die, but it was already too late. Anne was standing in front of her now.

"Oh, thank you." Beth turned her back towards Anne and let her unhook her bra and pull the straps down. Beth quickly crossed her arms over her now exposed breasts. She grabbed her shirt and pulled it on without turning around.

"Can I borrow a T-shirt?" Anne asked as she walked towards the bureau in just her underwear and bra. Beth had just a moment to stare at Anne's powerful legs. Each step revealed the parts that had always been covered by running shorts. They were the legs of an elite athlete. As Anne began to change, Beth realized she was still staring at her.

Beth laid down on her bed and reached for the bandage that was wrapped around her head, making sure it was still secure. She wasn't feeling much pain, perhaps due to the pain medication.

"Where should I sleep?" Anne asked as she stood over her looking down. Beth felt nervous and didn't know what to say.

"Chris won't mind if you use her bed. Besides, where else are you going to sleep?" Beth felt stupid as soon as it came out of her mouth.

"I was going to ask you to sleep on the floor because your bed looks more comfortable, and I think Chris's bed is full of crabs." She didn't change her tone of voice, but slowly a little smile snuck out.

Beth chuckled, but she couldn't come up with a good answer. She felt caught off guard. She secretly knew where she wanted Anne to sleep but couldn't imagine saying it out loud. Fortunately, Beth didn't have a choice, there was nowhere else to sleep.

"I guess I'll share mine, if you don't hog it." Beth couldn't believe Anne would be laying right next to her. It was only a full-size bed.

Anne hit the light switch and the room darkened.

"That will do," Anne joked.

Beth was still shocked. "I guess you're not kidding, are you?"

"Nope. Not after all you've told me about this roommate of yours. I certainly don't want to lay my body in her bed." Beth was laughing nervously as she moved over to make room for Anne. As Anne pulled back her side of the sheet and slid in, they both realized there was only one pillow.

"Oh my god…I'm so sorry Beth. You have a head full of stitches and here I am about to steal your pillow. I'll get Chris's." She started to sit up, but Beth suddenly feeling bolder, put her hand on Anne's shoulder and held her back, "No, no…that's okay. We can share. This pillow is extra wide, and you definitely don't want to use hers." Beth held her breath, hoping Anne would accept the offer.

"All right then, as long as you can get some sleep."

They laid on their backs with their eyes open, staring up at the dark ceiling. They were quiet. Beth could feel Anne's warm legs touching hers. She could smell her perfume, which she had grown to love. She was aware of the movement of Anne's chest as it rose and fell. She sensed her own breathing becoming deeper. Feeling Anne's body against her was appealing. She wanted to move closer. She was trying hard to figure out what Anne might be thinking. Was she the only one feeling this? She couldn't help picturing Anne's body stretched out next to her. It was arousing. She just laid still, wondering if Anne knew how she felt.

Suddenly, Anne turned on her side and raised up on her elbow and looked down at Beth. "Are you awake?" Anne asked breaking their silence.

"Yes…" Beth answered smiling as she looked up at Anne.

"You're probably going to think I'm crazy," she hesitated with apparent discomfort. "Damn…I feel like I'm the one who hit my head," she added with nervous sarcasm. "Beth…" she paused for a second, still staring at her, "Can I ask you something?"

Beth was dying with apprehension and curiosity. Her heart felt like it was pounding out of her chest.

"Yes," she said quietly.

Anne took a deep breath, "What are your feelings toward me?"

"What do you mean?" Beth panicked that Anne might have picked up on how she felt and tell her to leave her alone.

"Just that. What are you feeling about me?"

"Well…I think you're an amazing person." It took courage for her to even admit that.

"That's what you think." She emphasized the word 'think'. "I asked you about your feelings."

Although it seemed impossible, Beth's heart started to pound harder.

"Ohhh…how do I feel?" Beth drew out the word "feel." Anne just smiled at her. "I guess I feel very close to you. Actually, you're the best friend I have," she said nervously. Anne didn't say anything. Beth was afraid she had said too much. Maybe Anne didn't want to be best friends.

Beth returned the question. "So how do you feel about me?" She was filled with both fear and excitement as she waited for Anne's answer.

Anne turned away and laid her head back down on the pillow. She stared up at the ceiling and sighed. Then she almost whispered, "I don't want to scare you Beth, but I have to tell you…" she paused for just a moment, "I feel like I'm falling in love with you." Beth was stunned. Her body flushed with a new warmth and excitement. Those words gave her a feeling more beautiful and moving than anything she had ever felt or imagined. The euphoria felt surreal and paralyzing. Suddenly, without her control, tears started to roll down her cheeks. Anne turned and pulled her into her arms and held her. Beth was both embarrassed and overwhelmed with the feeling of love, as Anne embraced her. She felt safe in her arms and never wanted this feeling to stop.

"Anne..." Beth said softly. Anne released her embrace and moved back a little, so she could look at Beth's face. "I've never cared about anyone this much before. I think about you all the time. No one has ever made me happier." Then she paused. She was scared to tell the whole truth, and she was frightened that she might have misinterpreted what Anne meant by "falling in love". Beth couldn't get the words out. She laid there, trying to get her courage. Her voice seemed frozen, and her silence continued. She was just about to tell Anne how much she loved her, but she had waited too long. Anne slowly leaned forward and placed a lingering soft kiss on Beth's lips, then whispered, "You need to sleep now..."

Every part of Beth's body tingled. It was a feeling that was impossible to describe. She wanted more of Anne's kisses, but couldn't seem to speak or move. Anne pulled herself close to Beth and wrapped one arm over her. Beth felt overcome with emotion. She was afraid to sleep. She never wanted this moment to end, but she just couldn't find the words to tell her.

CHAPTER EIGHT

Broken Hearts

Beth didn't wake until later the next morning. It was nearly noon before she could manage to open her eyes. Her head was pounding, and she felt totally drained. Instantly, memories of the night flashed through her mind, only Anne was no longer lying by her side. The clothing that Anne had hung over the chair, was missing. In its place was Beth's neatly folded borrowed T-shirt. Beth knew she hadn't been dreaming. She could recollect the accident, the hospital, and everything that had happened in her room. It was all very clear. She couldn't understand why Anne left without saying goodbye. She felt disappointed but realized that she might be better off having some time to think. The time, however, was far more than Beth needed.

It was five days before she saw Anne again. Beth wasn't allowed to run, and Anne knew that, so why didn't she at least stop by? There was no contact at all, not even a phone call to see how her wound was healing. Beth desperately wanted to call Anne but was convinced that Anne didn't want to talk. Beth was confused, devastated and heart broken. She thought about Anne every waking moment. She couldn't figure out what was happening, or how to handle it. She questioned every moment of that night. Did Anne mean something different when she used the word "love"? Did she scare Anne away somehow? She tried to be rational, but nothing seemed to make sense, and nothing rid her of that empty, lonely feeling.

The first few days were the hardest because she couldn't run until she got the stitches out. She walked slowly to her classes looking at everyone, hoping one would be Anne. She went to the cafeteria, even though she wasn't hungry, in case Anne might be seated at one of the tables. She never asked any of Anne's friends if they had seen her around. She just couldn't do it. Beth was trying hard to forget, but she wasn't succeeding. She decided to remove her own stitches because she wouldn't ask anyone to take her to the doctor's. She felt the wound had closed tight enough, and since she couldn't run until they were out, she was going to make that happen. Beth wanted to run …she desperately needed to run. It was the only thing that could ease her heart ache.

Beth began running the cross-country course again. She punished herself with the pace. Her heart pounded so hard it helped dull her pain. She ran twice a day, once on the track and once on the cross-country course, but she never saw Anne. Several of the other runners who saw Beth, asked where Anne was. She would only tell them that she really didn't know. It was a truth that she hated to admit.

It was Saturday afternoon, and Beth was getting ready to go running. She had already run eight miles that morning and even though she was completely exhausted, she was going to run again. She decided that it would be a perfect test of her strength, both physical and mental. She was trying to prove something to herself and to Anne. She needed to prove that she was worthy…worthy of Anne's love.

As she rummaged through her drawers for fresh running clothes, there was a quiet, almost inaudible knock on the door. Beth had just taken off her shorts and T-shirt and she felt panicked, she didn't want anyone to just walk in. "Wait a minute," she called out, then as quickly as she could, she threw back on the clothing she had just taken off and opened the door. It was Anne. Neither spoke. They just stood there staring at each other. Beth's heart was racing.

"Hi Beth..." Anne said quietly, breaking the silence. Beth's emotions were muddled. She was so happy to see Anne again, and yet so angry and devastated.

"Long time no see," Beth said without emotion. She regretted it as soon as the words came out of her mouth. She couldn't hide her hurt, but she wanted to at least try.

"Yes...it has been," Anne said. She seemed uneasy. It was the first time Beth ever saw Anne without her air of confidence.

Beth couldn't speak for a moment. Her mind was too flooded with questions. Why did she just leave? Did she still feel the same? Did she know how much she hurt me? Should I just act like it was no big deal?

"Come in, I'm sorry, I didn't mean to make you stand out in the hall," Beth finally said.

"Thanks," Anne said sounding relieved as she entered. She looked at Beth as she walked in and a strange smile came over her. It was the type of smile one has after just playing a joke on someone. As she sat down on the bed, Anne asked with a satirical tone, "Were you going running?" Beth didn't think anything was funny right now.

"Yeah, I was just getting ready when you knocked."

"You must be in an awful hurry," she said as she signaled for Beth to look down at herself.

"Oh shit..." Beth mumbled as a little grin broke through her stoic face. In her rush to get to the door, she had put her T-shirt on backwards, and her shorts inside out.

Beth began to laugh, and Anne joined her. The laughter helped ease the tension.

"Is there any way I can talk you out of running, at least until tomorrow?" Anne asked, sounding hopeful that Beth might say yes.

"Oh my god...I better not go running, at least not until I learn to dress myself," she joked, shaking her head in disbelief.

"Good, then would you consider going someplace with me tonight?" Anne asked seeming a little unsure of herself.

"All right, as long as it's legal," Beth said, thinking immediately how corny it sounded. She was uncomfortable and struggling to act as if everything was normal. Earlier in the week she thought she would be cold and indifferent to Anne, but she just couldn't do it. Just seeing her, kindled her attraction and desire to hold her.

"Don't worry, it's legal but it's not going to be much fun," Anne said as if she were giving Beth a chance to back out.

"What did you want to do?"

"Well, I'm going home to see my Mom. She's in the hospital for a hysterectomy. They operate tomorrow morning and I think she's scared about it. I figured I'd go and cheer her up. I thought I'd ask you to go, so you can meet my family and they can see what nice all-American friends I've met in college."

"Oh, is that what you think I am, the all-American type?" she asked with a little smirk. Beth's mind, however, was resisting the urge to tell Anne that she didn't have the right to call her "friend", not after she just abandoned her.

75

"Well, what if I disappoint them?"

"You won't," Anne said confidently.

"All right, I'll go. I would like to meet your family. I have to see what made you the way you are." Beth realized after she said it, that that statement could be interpreted several different ways.

"Great, I'm so glad you're coming," Anne said like she truly meant it.

"But…you better put different clothes on, or at least put yours on the right way. Remember, I'm using you for a good impression." They both laughed, but still seemed a little uneasy with each other.

"I must look pretty good, huh?" Beth joked.

Anne maintained eye contact and said softy, but seriously, "Yes…you do, you look beautiful." There was no teasing in her voice. Beth felt those familiar butterflies but tried to ignore them.

"When are we leaving?"

"Right now."

As Beth quickly changed, she sensed Anne watching her. She knew that Anne was just pretending to read the book that she had just grabbed off the desk.

"There, I'm ready," Beth said as she tied the final bow on her sneakers.

"Good, let's go." Anne grabbed Beth's arm and pulled her towards the door, as though she couldn't wait another second longer. She hit the light switch as she gently pushed Beth out of the room, then closed the door behind them.

"We've got to hurry. I'm doubled parked," Anne yelled as they started running down the hall. When they got outside, Beth saw a convertible MG with its flashers on.

"Is this yours? Where's your BMW?"

"I just borrowed it from a guy I know. Mine's in the shop".

"Wow...you must have some trusting friends," Beth said as she shook her head.

"No ticket," Anne cheered. "I can relax now. You know how the campus police are. They'll get you for anything they can because they don't have anything else to do."

They got in, and Anne turned off the flashers and put the roof down. It was a clear autumn afternoon. Anne started the car and raced the engine. She bragged mockingly, that it sounded just like a race car. She seemed to be herself again. It was clear however, that Anne was going to act like nothing had happened. Beth was still angry and upset and wanted explanations.

"Do you know where my home is?" Anne asked.

"You told me the name of the town, but I don't really know where it is."

"Well, the truth is, I decided to get you in the car before I told you that it'll take us about three hours to get there." Anne looked at Beth and cringed a little, "I'm sorry I should have told you, but I didn't want you to say no."

"I don't care. I had nothing better to do tonight." Her tone was apathetic, but her heart felt otherwise. She cared. She cared deeply that she didn't have answers or apologies. It was frustrating, but she was determined to wait until Anne spoke first...if she ever did.

As Anne drove, they made small talk. It seemed that whenever there might be a moment of silence, one of them would throw in a question or comment to keep a conversation going. They both seemed strangely uncomfortable with any silence.

After about an hour, Anne asked Beth if she would like to drive the car.

"I can't drive stick," Beth said disappointedly. Anne pulled off the road and said, "Now's the time to learn."

"This isn't even your car."

"That's okay. He won't mind. I'll make sure we're safe".

Anne jumped out of the car and ran over to Beth's side. Beth got out and climbed in behind the steering wheel.

"I'll probably ruin the car," she said as she placed her hand on the gear shift.

"No, you won't. I promise. Just push the clutch in."

As Beth pushed it in, Anne placed her hand on top of Beth's. Beth was very aware of her touch and cherished it.

"These are the gears," she said guiding Beth's hand around the H shape.

"You can do it. Just let the clutch out easy as you press the gas pedal. Got it?"

"I think so."

"Good, let's go," Anne said with apparent confidence in Beth's ability. There was a noticeable jerk when Beth first pulled back onto the road. Otherwise, she handled the car with no trouble.

Beth was so focused on driving, that her mind finally had a chance to think about something other than Anne. With only a few miles to go, Anne congratulated Beth on her ability to drive stick shift. "I'm impressed. I really am. You picked this up faster than anyone I know." There was a pause, "I keep telling you Beth, there's just something special about you…I just feel it," she said shaking her head and looking at her. Beth chose not to look over or to respond. She just kept her eyes on the road.

"Turn left here and when you get to those two round reflectors sticking up on the right, turn up that little driveway," Anne instructed.

"You're kidding! You mean there's a house somewhere back in these woods?"

"I sure hope so," Anne kidded.

Beth turned into the driveway. It was a long winding dirt road with woods on either side.

"I don't even see a house yet!" Beth said in disbelief.

"It's back here, keep going."

Finally, they reached a modern wooden structure surrounded by a landscape of trees and bushes instead of a grass lawn. Beth pulled into a gravel parking area next to the house and turned off the car. Her mouth dropped open as she looked around.

"This is beautiful!"

"Ahhh…it just looks that way because the sun is setting," Anne said modestly. Beth began to feel uncomfortable. She hadn't realized how well-to-do Anne was. Beth's brother was not as financially stable by any means. In fact, they often struggled to make ends meet. "Nobody is home yet. Want to look around before it gets dark? It's really pretty this time of the year." Anne led her back through the autumn colored trees.

"How long have you lived here?"

Since I was nine. We used to live in Florida. I think I like it better here though. I just wish we had some neighbors. The closest one is two miles away. I didn't have anyone to play with." She paused and added, "It would've been really cool if we were friends when we were young."

"That might've been nice," Beth said, "but I was a real tomboy. You probably would have hated me. I would have built a treehouse in every tree."

"Why do you think I wouldn't like a tomboy? I was one too! As a matter of fact, I still am and I'm not ashamed of it," Anne said half smiling at what seemed to be an insult to her. "Come with me, let me show you something," she said leading her down a worn path to a huge tree. "Look!" she said as she pointed up to a sturdy treehouse sitting in the old oak tree. "I built that just two summers ago. See? I'm still a tomboy."

"All right, I'm sorry. I figured you for the type that spent most of your time choosing a new boyfriend to bring back here."

"Thanks a lot. I thought you thought more of me than that," Anne said sounding almost serious. Beth didn't realize she had offended Anne. She had been a little jealous of those types of girls anyway.

"No, that's not what I mean…" Beth said with frustration. She just didn't know how to express it.

80

"Never mind, if you don't know how much I really think of you by now, I guess you never will." The words just came out. It wasn't premeditated, it just happened. They stared at each other. Anne's eyes became watery as she looked down. Beth couldn't hold her thoughts in anymore. "Damn it Anne! Where were you all week?" Anne's head lifted quickly. She looked surprised.

"Beth, I'm sorry...My God, I thought you might be glad. I thought I frightened you. You don't know how much I wanted to call you."

"Well, why didn't you?"

Anne took a deep breath and looked away for a moment as she gathered her thoughts. "I was too scared. What I'm feeling is so different from anything else I have ever felt for anyone. I didn't know if I should've ever told you that I was falling in love. I didn't know if I should've kissed you either. You're so innocent, and I honestly couldn't tell if being with another woman was even a possibility for you. How could I? You didn't tell me...I swear though I never wanted to hurt you. That's the last thing I would ever want to do to you. My heart was breaking not being with you."

Beth was silent. She just stood there watching Anne's blond hair blow around in a soft breeze. She wanted to reach out and hold this beautiful woman. Anne continued to look at Beth and questioned, "Beth...if you felt this way, why didn't you call me?"

Beth paused, "I couldn't. I was too hurt that you left without saying anything. I just couldn't do it. I didn't think you wanted to talk to me anyway. You just disappeared. I figured I must have done something wrong. I kept asking myself if I had shared too much with you. Or maybe I didn't say the right things. I wasn't sure that I was interpreting what you said accurately. I was honestly trying to tell you how I felt, but I couldn't get the words out before you kissed me and told me to go to sleep. My head and heart were spinning. I couldn't speak."

"You can speak now, can't you?" Anne said softly as she stared into Beth's eyes. Beth was holding back tears. "Anne…I've been in love with you for a long time. I've never been so in love. I don't know what I'm supposed to do."

"Do your feelings frighten you?"

"Yes…I guess they do," she said quietly, looking down.

Anne placed her hand under Beth's chin, and raised Beth's head so they could look directly into each other's eyes.

"Why? We can't change how we feel. That's something we have no control over. We shouldn't feel guilty."

Beth looked at Anne as the colorful dry leaves blew around their feet and the sky grew darker. They stood silently, as though neither of them knew what to say or do. Beth walked over to a large log resting on the ground and sat down.

"Shit…I wish I were a guy right now, at least I'd know what I'm supposed to do," Beth mumbled. Anne came over and sat down next to her. Beth was looking out towards the woods, but she could feel Anne looking at her.

"Why? What can't you do now that you could do if you were a guy?" Beth could feel her body flush with warmth. She was nervous, and her body was trembling inside. She believed Anne knew exactly what she was talking about. Beth looked over at Anne, and saw her watching her mouth, waiting for the answer. Beth took a deep breath and said, "Kiss you." Neither moved. They stared silently at each other. Beth's eyes lowered and focused on Anne's soft pink lips, that were tempting her, exciting every part of her body. She never felt such a powerful urge. She slowly raised her hands and placed them on either side of Anne's face. She pulled Anne close. Anne didn't resist. Suddenly, a nearby voice called out, "Anne, Anne, is that you back there?" They jumped spontaneously and Beth pulled her hands away, panicking. Anne's father was near, but hopefully not close enough to have seen them. Anne looked disappointedly at Beth before she said, "Yeah Dad…just me and a friend."

"Okay, just wanted to make sure that was your car parked out front. I thought you might be back here showing off your tree house," he said as he started to approach.

"Don't worry Dad, we'll be right up, and I'll properly introduce you to one of my good friends."

"All right, I look forward to meeting you," he said smiling at Beth. Then he turned and started walking back toward the house.

"Thank you." Beth could barely get the words out.

"Oh shit Beth…I am so sorry! He scared me half to death. My heart is beating so hard I can hear it."

Beth's own heart was pounding frantically, from both the excitement and the interruption. Anne looked at Beth and said softly, "We better go." Beth walked by Anne's side through the darkening woods. Neither spoke, but Anne reached down and took Beth's hand, and held it gently as they walked slowly back to the house.

CHAPTER NINE

First Real Kiss

"Hi Dad," Anne said as she entered her very tastefully furnished house. "I'd like you to meet someone. This is Beth, a very close friend of mine from school." Still shaking, Beth smiled and said, "Glad to meet you." Anne's father was a perfect match for the word "handsome". He had a full head of light brown hair, blue eyes, was tall, very fit, and sported a welcoming smile.

"It's a pleasure to have you in our home," he said with a comfortable cheerfulness. "Are you the runner who's going to break those college track records? I've heard a lot about you from Anne, and she doesn't praise too many people. You must be very special to her."

"Well…I don't know about that but thank you very much anyway."

"You're welcome. Now…let's get ready to go to the hospital. Visiting hours are short so I'd like to get there early. Beth, I assume you're going with us. I'm sure Anne's mother would love to meet you."

Within minutes, they were in the car and heading toward the hospital. Anne sat in the front seat with her father. Whenever Beth was involved in the conversation, Anne would look back at her and give her a smile that seemed to be intentionally seductive. It made Beth's heart race. She couldn't wait to be alone with Anne.

Anne and her father checked in at the front desk and then ran to the gift shop to buy flowers. When they got to the room and Beth first saw Anne's mother, she knew immediately from which side of the family Anne got her good looks. Anne's mother was tall and thin like Anne, but her blond hair was not quite as light. Their faces were similarly structured, and their smiles were almost identical.

She was a picture of Anne in about twenty years…attractive, healthy, and youthful looking. Anne's mother was charming. She was quieter than Anne's father, but still very friendly. Beth felt comfortable talking with Anne's mother, but being with Anne was all she could think about.

After a pleasant visit and reassurance that her Mom was going to be fine, they returned to the Stetson's home.

Back at the house, Beth, Anne, and Anne's father sat around the kitchen table and discussed a variety of subjects. Track of course was a big part of it, but it also included amusing childhood stories about Anne. After a while, her dad noticed the time and announced, "Looks like you girls will have to stay overnight. It's too late to leave now."

"No, we'll be fine," Anne insisted.

"I would feel a lot better if you stayed. We'll make room." Anne didn't want to disappoint her father, but she didn't know how Beth felt about staying.

"It's really up to you Beth." Beth was caught off guard and a little flustered.

"Oh…whatever you want to do is fine with me."

"Are you sure?" Anne observed Beth for clues indicating what she honestly wanted to do.

"Really…It's fine with me. We can stay." Beth really wasn't sure what to say, and she couldn't tell what Anne was thinking.

"Good, good! You can take Anne's old room and Anne can sleep in the study. There should be some clean sheets already on the bed, so just make yourself at home.

Beth hadn't thought about where she would sleep. She knew she just wanted to be with Anne.

"Thanks Dad, I'll make sure she's comfortable."

"Yes, thank you Mr. Stetson," Beth said forcing a smile. It wasn't that she didn't appreciate his hospitality, she just couldn't think clearly about anything. She was consumed with the anticipation of being with Anne.

"Well Dad, I think we'll go to bed now, so we can get up and run tomorrow morning, before we see Mom," Anne placed a little kiss on her father's cheek. Meanwhile, Beth was thinking she didn't have her running sneakers, nor did she even have anything to sleep in.

"Okay, good night and don't let the bedbugs bite!" he said as he fluffed Anne's hair. Beth had a sudden flashback…that was exactly what her father used to do.

"Good night Dad," Anne said with a smirk, acknowledging her dad's corny comment. Then she grabbed Beth's arm and guided her to the steps.

When they got upstairs, Anne offered her something to sleep in and gave her a new toothbrush. Beth sensed that Anne might not want the immediate privacy she did, but then she was often wrong about what was going on in Anne's mind. Maybe Anne thought her dad could still hear them. She seemed nervous, but Beth couldn't imagine Anne being nearly as nervous as she was. Anne showed Beth to the guest bathroom. Beth changed, cleaned up, and brushed her teeth. When she came out of the bathroom, Anne was standing there already changed. Her strong legs were scarcely covered by black cotton gym shorts, and a pair of sweat socks, which only came up to where her calf muscles bulged out. "Come on, I'll show you your room.

By the way, I do have a pair of running sneakers that will fit you, since we take the same size. Tomorrow, we'll have a chance to run together through the woods. Just the two of us..." Anne said as she gave Beth a warm suggestive smile. That smile made Beth's heart race.

Beth followed Anne down the hallway. "Is this okay?" she asked as she flicked on the lights in the room. "I'll be right down the hall if you need anything," she said looking directly into Beth's warm brown eyes. Beth wasn't sure if Mr. Stetson could hear them, so she whispered as she reached out and touched Anne's arm, "I need to talk to you."

"Beth, if it's okay with you, I'd like to come back after my father goes to bed." It seemed as if she thought Beth might say no.

"Oh my God Anne...of course it's all right. Why would you even ask that?" Beth said still whispering.

"Just wanted to make sure you didn't change your mind..." Anne said quietly then smiled as she reached down and squeezed Beth's hand. Beth felt a warm sensation run through her body.

Beth looked around the room, trying to imagine Anne growing up in it. There was everything a perfect little child should have. There were books, a microscope, and educational charts on one side. On the other side sat a set of old weights. Beth got a kick out of that, and it helped explain why Anne had become such a great student-athlete. It seemed Anne had everything that Beth had only dreamed of having...a big house, a car, extra money, talent, and parents.

Beth walked over to the window and opened it just enough to let in the brisk autumn air. She stood there enjoying the smells and the goose bumps it gave her. Finally, she turned off the lights and climbed into fresh sheets. She waited anxiously, wondering how long it would be before Mr. Stetson would go to bed. She couldn't believe this day was real. Was this just a wonderful dream, from which she'd have to wake up? Several minutes passed. Beth listened to the crickets outside, and the sound of the crisp leaves rustling as the breeze blew through their branches. Finally, she heard movement downstairs. Soon there were footsteps walking up the stairway. They faded as they headed down the hallway to the master bedroom.

Beth was wide awake now, and nervous with excitement. Finally, the door slowly opened. Anne slipped in the room and closed it quietly behind her. Beth sat up in bed.

"Hi," Anne whispered.

"Hi," Beth replied softly but her heart was pounding with energy. Anne walked over to the bed and sat down on the edge of it facing Beth. "How do you like this room?" she said quietly.

"It's fine but I'd rather be sharing one," Beth responded, surprising herself. Anne smiled warmly back at her. Beth could see Anne's stunning face from the moonlight coming in the window. She couldn't believe that this beautiful woman loved her. She felt elated but uneasy. They were both quiet for a moment. Anne reached over and placed her warm soft hand on top of Beth's. Beth's body trembled with excitement. Beth turned her hand over, and they intertwined fingers. Anne slowly lifted Beth's hand to her lips and kissed it softly. Beth watched Anne's face. Her heart was beating wildly. Their eyes locked. "God, I love you Beth," Anne said tenderly. She placed another gentle kiss on Beth's hand. Beth shook her head in disbelief and whispered, "I just can't believe I'm here with you…my body is shaking. See what you're doing to me?"

"Good…because you're having the same effect on me," Anne said as she let go of Beth's hand, reached out, and gently took Beth's face in her hands. Her eyes lowered and focused on Beth's lips, as she pulled her slowly towards her. Beth's entire body awakened. She closed her eyes and felt the soft yet insistent warmth of Anne's lips on her mouth. The excitement almost weakened her. She lifted her arms and reached behind Anne, pulling her closer. Beth had never experienced such a sensuous response like this, from a kiss. She wanted more, but Anne pulled away and said sincerely, "Beth, I've got to make sure you know what you're doing." Beth almost laughed, "I think it's called kissing, isn't it?" Anne just smiled at her.

"Can you stay here tonight?" Beth whispered. Anne looked at her for another moment, then placed her hands on Beth's shoulders and gently pushed her back, so that her head was on the pillow.

"Yes…" she said quietly as she pulled the covers back and slipped in next to Beth. Then she turned over and lowered herself down on top of her. Beth could feel the warmth of Anne's body even through her shirt. She could feel Anne's breasts gently touching hers. She wrapped her dark muscular arms around Anne, and pulled her closer, then began kissing her lips softly. Their lips parted and their kisses grew more intimate. Beth's desire grew as

Anne began to softly kiss her way up to Beth's ear lobe. Beth couldn't take it. She took Anne's head and guided it back to her mouth and kissed her with passion. Her hands reached under the covers and touched the back of Anne's long legs. She moved her hands softly and slowly up Anne's body and over its curvatures, until her hands were resting in the small of Anne's back. She slipped her hands under Anne's shirt and delicately allowed her fingers to move up her back, feeling the softness and strength. Anne slowly turned on her side, bringing Beth with her. She slipped one leg between Beth's, and gently kissed her. Beth felt the pressure between her thighs and her excitement grew stronger. She wanted to feel Anne's skin on hers. She wanted to explore and touch every part of Anne's beautiful body. She wanted Anne to touch her too, but she wasn't sure what the rules were. Was it too soon?

"Anne," Beth whispered, looking into her eyes, "I just can't get close enough to you. I want to feel every part of your body, but I don't know if you want me to."

"Oh, believe me Beth...I want you to," she whispered with a little smile. "I want you to touch me more than you can imagine. I'm dying here... you have me so excited I can barely hold myself back," she said making light of her sexual frustration. Then more seriously, "I really don't want to rush you though. This is your first time, at least with a woman, so I think we should take it slow, besides," she smiled, "my father is a few doors down from us, and I'm worried he'll hear me if we go any further."

"Oh my God Anne...my mind might agree with you, but my body sure doesn't," Beth teased quietly.

They held and kissed each other until nearly dawn. The time had gone by unnoticed. They had fallen asleep with Anne's head resting on Beth's chest, and Beth's arm wrapped around her. As the sun started to shine through the window, Anne opened her eyes and sat up. "Beth...Beth," she said in a whisper as she gently shook one shoulder. Beth looked up and saw Anne propped up on her elbow, gazing down at her. Now that it was daylight, she felt almost embarrassed about the intimate night they had shared.

"I've got to go back to my room before my father gets up," she whispered as she got out of bed.

"Okay," Beth said quietly. Anne leaned over and kissed her lightly on her lips. Familiar feelings stirred her memories. Anne got up and walked towards the door, "You better get what sleep you can, we are going to run before we go see my Mom."

"Yes ma'am," she whispered, saluting Anne as she snuck out the door.

CHAPTER TEN

The Pond

Later that morning, Mr. Stetson went upstairs and knocked quietly on Anne's door.

"Come in," Anne said drowsily.

"Wake up honey. I have breakfast ready for you downstairs." Anne forced her eyes open and looked at her father.

"Okay Dad, I'll get Beth up. We'll be down shortly."

"All right honey. It's an absolutely beautiful day, so take advantage of it. I'm going to see your Mom after you head off for your run, but she doesn't want any other company until after lunch, so you'll have some time to relax."

Within fifteen minutes the three of them were sitting around the table eating scrambled eggs, and an array of fresh fruit. Beth was still trying to wake up. She was feeling the effects of the night. Anne was rather quiet while she ate her breakfast.

"Boy, you two look exhausted. Didn't either of you sleep well last night?"

"I guess it was the strange beds," Anne suggested. Then behind her father's back, she gave Beth a big grin.

"Well, maybe you can take naps before you come over to see your mom."

"We'll recover, don't worry," she said as she stood up and went over to put her plate in the sink. Then she patted him on the back and said, "That was perfect Dad. If I eat any more, I won't be able to run."

"Thank you, Mr. Stetson. This was delicious but I don't think I can eat anymore either," she said as she got up patting her belly.

"'Let me have your plate Beth, so I can wash it,'" Anne said.

"Oh no, I'll take care of the dishes," Mr. Stetson asserted. "You two go get ready for your run."

"Okay, thanks Dad, I owe you one."

Anne and Beth went upstairs to change into their running outfits, which consisted of anything Anne could find in her bureau drawers. Beth went downstairs first and was soon joined by Anne.

"Why do you have a backpack?" Beth asked Anne when she saw it in her hand.

"I usually carry it when I run through the woods. I have something special in it," she teased. Beth just smiled and didn't bother to ask what.

The September morning was warmer than normal. Anne began leading the run along the dirt paths, dodging trees, jumping over fallen logs, and noisily crushing the colorful leaves beneath her sneakers. It was a beautiful bright sunny day, and Beth fell into the euphoria that runners often feel after they have been running for a while. Combined with the excitement stirred by the memories of night, Beth was filled with pure bliss.

They ran at a comfortable pace without talking until they reached a small clearing.

"Let's stop here and cool down a little. I want to show you something," Anne announced. Beth didn't notice anything at first, until Anne started walking towards the trees that surrounded the clearing. Then she noticed a welcoming pond, just behind the trees.

"This is my hidden treasure and I wanted to share it with you."

"Oh my god, this is beautiful! Are we still on your property?"

"Yes…I guess I could say, it's all ours."

"Have you ever gone in?" Beth asked, genuinely curious.

"That's why I brought you here. I think we should go for a little swim to cool off. I do it all the time during the summer. No one is around. It's completely private."

"Really?" Beth asked surprised. "Do you go in with your running clothes on?"

"Not really…" Anne said teasingly, allowing Beth a moment to figure it out.

"No way! You go skinny dipping here? I could never do that!"

"Why not? No one will see us."

"No way…"

"I'll make you a compromise…how about we go in our underwear? It's no different than our usual running outfits." Beth didn't have a good rebuttal.

"Come on, I know you'll love it. That's why I have the knapsack. It has towels and dry clothing. Come on Beth…you'll love it."

Although Beth was a good swimmer, she asked, "How deep is it?"

"It's not deep…maybe four feet."

"How cold is it?"

"We'll have to find out," Anne said as she pulled off her T-shirt and shorts. Then she went over to Beth and said with a seductive grin, "Let me help you…" Beth smiled and let Anne help her pull off her shirt.

They stood there looking like two models in their silk panties and bras. Anne's were black, and Beth's were white. It highlighted the contrast of these two young women, who had so much in common, and yet were so different.

Anne grabbed Beth's hand and said, "On the count of three, ready?"

"No wait…are we jumping or diving?"

"We can do shallow dives. It will come up to just below your chest. You can dive, can't you?"

"Yes," she said smirking, as if she had been insulted. "I was a lifeguard every summer when I was in high school. I bet you were one too. At least you looked it the first time I saw you."

"My…how observant you are. You must have been checking me out," she kidded.

"Well …I guess I was," she joked back with a suggestive smile.

"Well…maybe you can check me out more when we get in the water," she teased. Anne then took Beth's hand, and pulled her to the edge of the water where they dove in with barely a splash. They both came up at the same time laughing, then started jumping up and down to keep warm. The water was cold but not frigid. The sun on the pond and the warm September days, had helped heat it. The water sparkled on their still tanned faces, and their wet hair, pulled back in ponytails, shone in the sun.

"I didn't expect it to be this cold!" Beth yelled, laughing at the same time.

"You'll get used to it," Anne laughed. Beth's thin white bra showed how cold the water truly was. Beth continued to hop around, until Anne reached out and took Beth's arms, and drew her towards her. She wrapped her arms around Beth, but instead of the warm embrace that Beth expected, Anne pulled her down under the water. Beth came back up laughing and began splashing Anne with the cold pond water. Then she grabbed Anne and tried to submerge her, without much success. They were laughing and playing so hard they couldn't talk. When they finally stopped, Anne looked at the sweet smile on Beth's face and pulled her again into her arms. She gently kissed her lips and Beth no longer noticed the temperature of the water. She could only feel her own temperature rise. Beth returned the kiss with the feelings that had been building inside. Anne released one hand and reached behind Beth and unhooked her bra. Anne slowly moved the straps off Beth's shoulders and slid them all the way down her arms. As the bra came off, it revealed a body that most women would die for. Anne pulled her tight against her and kissed her neck. Beth felt the excitement as she reached around Anne's back and released her bra, allowing it to slide into the water. She looked at Anne's half naked figure. She found it flawless and beautiful. The type painters dream of painting. It was sensual, alluring and stimulated her desire even more. Beth pulled Anne tight against her in an embrace that was more sexual than the tender ones she usually gave. She could feel Anne's body securely against her. She still wanted to feel more.

"You are so damn beautiful," Beth said as she stepped back a little and very gently placed her hands on Anne's breast.

Anne smiled at Beth and said seductively, "You're the sexiest woman I know. Damn…you turn me on just looking at you." Beth didn't say anything. She lowered her head and put her lips on Anne's breasts.

"Oh Christ Beth…" Anne whispered as she closed her eyes and leaned her head back.

As Beth's urge for sexual closeness grew, she sought more. She pulled Anne's face close and kissed her with pure passion. She lost herself in the feeling of love, and raw sexuality. She felt Anne's hand starting to slide down her body. Beth's excitement intensified and she didn't want Anne to stop. She felt Anne's soft touch, slowly slide down under her wet underwear. Beth gasped when Anne's fingers delicately touched her most sensitive areas. Her body started to quiver. Suddenly, Anne stopped and looked around with panic in her eyes. She said quietly, "Did you hear something?" Beth was still lost in the moment and had to focus hard to understand what Anne said.

"What?" she barely uttered.

"Oh Shit…I thought I heard someone!" she whispered frantically. Beth's eyes widened. She listened closely. She heard it too. It was at least two men. They were close enough that you could almost hear their conversation.

"Fuck! Oh fuck! What the hell are we supposed to do?" Beth whispered in a panic.

"Quick…swim to the other side. We can hide in the woods!" Anne directed decisively.

"What about our clothing?" Beth said still panicking.

"Too late now! Go! Go! Go!" Anne demanded.
They swam quickly to the other side, climbed up the small embankment and ran into the trees. They ran in their bare feet with nothing on but their underwear. Beth crossed her arms over her breasts to both hide them and stop them from bouncing.

"OK, here, behind this tree," Anne said quietly.

"I can't fucking believe this…" Beth whispered in Anne's ear as she stood behind her.

They could now see two males with hunting rifles on the other side the pond. They were heading towards the backpack, and the scattered clothes Beth and Anne had left behind.

"Look Dad, I think someone is here," the teenage boy said as he picked up the knapsack and peaked in. "This is girl's stuff. Looks like two of them were here."

"Put that down, now! We shouldn't even be here. We need to get out of here."

"But Dad, what if something is wrong? What if they're hurt or kidnapped or something? Should we call 911?" he said nervously.

"No, no…" His father said, trying to figure out what to do.

"Is anybody here? Are you all right?" He yelled loudly, then waited for a response.

"Do you need help?"

Anne looked at Beth and whispered, "I've got to let them know we're here, or they might call 911."

"You guys need to leave this property now! I almost shot you. There's no hunting on my property," Anne hollered back.

"Yes Ma'am. We're very sorry. We got lost."

"Well, you have no excuses now. Just turn around and follow the path out of here," she yelled angrily.

"We're really sorry," he hollered back, then looked at his son and said quietly,

"Let's get the hell out of here."

When the hunters were out of sight, the two half naked girls, looking like beautiful nymphs hiding behind the foliage, looked at each other in shock and then started laughing.

"I can't believe this happened! This is crazy! Are you sure they're gone? Do you think they saw us? What do we do now?" Beth rattled on.

Anne could not get the wide grin off her face, "Can you imagine the sight they would have seen if we hadn't heard them? That would be something they would never forget, especially for that boy. Can you imagine him telling his friends he saw two pretty, shirtless girls, making out in the middle of a pond... hmm, lot of wet dreams for that kid."

"Oh my God, what a story! How sad that we won't be able to tell anybody!" Beth said still behind the tree with her arms wrapped around herself.

Anne continued to laugh as she said, "I'm still shaking! I don't know if it's from the cold or from what just happened, but we need to get back."

"Do we have to get in that cold water again?" Beth complained.

"If we had clothing and shoes, we could walk around, but since we don't, we're swimming!"

Beth begrudgingly walked towards the water. Suddenly she stopped, looked at Anne and laughed out loud, "Oh my God! Is that my bra floating on a stick?"

On the way back to the house they held hands, except when they stopped to exchange passionate kisses. Since Anne's father would be at the hospital, they decided they would take advantage of the empty house and a warm bed. They were longing to be intimate again.

When they reached the house, Anne's father's car was parked in the driveway.

"Oh my god…my father's home," Anne said with utter disappointment.

Beth's heart sank as she said woefully, "I guess, this spoils our plans, doesn't it?"

"I'm so sorry Beth, I don't know what to say. You don't know how frustrating this is. I just want to be alone with you someplace," she said looking into Beth's eyes. "I really want to make love to you Beth," then added grinning, "but in a bed." Beth smiled back at her and whispered, "You'll be my first…"

It turned out that Anne's mother was feeling well enough to have company, sooner rather than later. She didn't want the girls to have to drive back in the dark, so she sent Anne's father home to get them.

Beth and Anne cleaned up and changed their clothing. They decided it would be best to follow Anne's father to the hospital and leave from there. After a pleasant visit, they said their goodbyes and headed back to college, tired and in love.

CHAPTER ELEVEN

Try Outs with Coach Ryan

Anne picked Beth up at her dorm, and they drove over to the track for the first day of tryouts. They had been training hard. They spent hours on the cross-country course, aiming to increase endurance, and to improve the strength of their already powerful legs. They ran on the track every other day, trying to find the best pace for the mile run. Beth was prepared, but that didn't stop her from being anxious.

As they walked up to the track, Beth saw that Carol was already there warming up. She knew Carol was going to be on the track team, but she never thought about having to run against her.

"I see Carol over there," Beth said without emotion as she pointed her out.

"Oh good, I'm glad she showed up," Anne said casually.

"Did she ever say she didn't want to go out?" Beth asked surprised.

"The last time I spoke to her, she said she's worried that you might take her spot on the team."

"What?" Beth said loudly, obviously surprised. "When did she say that?"

"I'm just kidding you…but I know she's worried that you can beat her. When she called me last week, she said she was surprised that you were such a strong runner."

Beth didn't know that they had talked to each other. She wondered how often they spoke. She knew it shouldn't bother her because they're just friends, but it did.

"Well…I hope I live up to her expectations, but I know she won't be happy when I actually do," she said with a confident little grin as they walked over to join the rest of the group. The confidence wasn't genuine.

"Hey Anne...come sit over here with me," Carol said as she waved them over. Beth wasn't fond of the idea but followed along.

"Hi Beth, I'm glad you're here. I guess we'll all be going out for the mile positions, so we might as well sit together," she joked.

"All right everybody, listen up!" Coach Sandy Ryan yelled. "We're going to break up into two groups. All people trying out for any field events, such as shot put, high jump, pole vault, discus, and javelin, meet me over there," she announced as she pointed to a large, marked area on the field.

"I will send someone over shortly to start working with you. In the meantime, you can stretch out a little more or start your own warm-ups." She waited patiently as more than a couple dozen girls picked up their gym bags and headed to their station. Coach Ryan then turned back to the group of girls nearly twice as large.

"Now...for you runners, we're going to start out today with a timed mile run." There were a few moans, mostly by the upperclassmen. The newcomers were too nervous to say anything, especially Beth.

"Now I know some of you won't be milers, but it gives me a good chance to see what type of running material we have here," she said as she looked around the group.

"I see a few new faces here who I really don't know anything about," she admitted as she glanced at Beth and a few other girls. "In two days, we'll determine if you have what we're looking for." Beth's stomach was in a knot already, now it just got worse.

"We'll run in four heats…Juniors and Seniors in the first two heats, and Freshman and Sophomores in the second two. I'll have somebody calling out splits on every lap. Just in case you don't know this, you need to run four laps around this quarter mile track." Some of the girls laughed.

"Freshman and Sophomores, check the list and see what heat you're in." Beth and Carol were amongst the many girls who walked over to the large posters with the runner's names on it. Beth found her name, then quickly looked for Carol's. They were in the same heat. They would go in the second group.

"Okay, everybody up and over to the starting line." A few of the runners took a last-minute stretch. Beth and Carol walked over to watch the upper classman. Anne stood quickly and grabbed Beth by the arm before she could get too far away. She whispered, "Don't be nervous. Just do your best. You got this Beth."

"At least I don't have to run against the seniors," Beth said trying to find something to ease her nervousness.

"Ms. Ryan is just looking at times to see potential. It's only the first day. She doesn't expect miracles, especially if you're only a freshman. Now relax, will you?" Anne smiled encouragingly as she placed her hands on Beth's shoulder, and shook her a little. Anne's touch caused Beth to flash a brief memory of the intimate touching they had the day before.

Coach Ryan walked up to Anne and asked, "Anne, will you do me a favor? I need you to call out their splits. I'll get your mile time tomorrow if you don't mind."

"Sure, I'd be glad to," Anne offered politely as she took the stopwatch.

"Thanks. You can go get set up now. I'm going to start them very shortly."

"Okay," Anne said as she started walking away. Then she turned back and caught both Beth's and Carol's attention, "Good luck! Run hard you two."

The first heat of the juniors and seniors went off smoothly. Beth and Carol sat next to each other on the side of the track, stretching out their muscular legs as the runners went by.

"Wow…they look fast," Beth told Carol.

"Don't worry, they'll start slowing down at the halfway point. Most of those girls are sprinters," Carol said knowingly. Her insights helped Beth relax a little.

"Good job…Good job," coach Ryan called out encouragingly as the runners struggled across the finish line. Carol was right, many of them had burned themselves out before the last quarter mile. This proved true on the second heat as well.

"Next group up…Freshman and Sophomores…take your positions!" Coach yelled as the last girl finished. Beth walked to the starting line and shook both her arms and legs out. Carol stood right next to her and did the same.

"Is everybody relaxed and ready?" coach Ryan asked warmly as she aimed her gun in the air.

Some of the girls shook their heads affirmatively and others just smiled nervously.

"Runners take your mark, get set…" then the gun went off with a jolting bang.

Most of the runners took off at a sprinters pace, trying to get to the inside lane. Beth passed enough girls to put herself in fifth place. Carol came up behind her. Beth didn't think the pace felt that hard. On the first lap, when she ran past Anne, who was calling out their times, she could hear her yelling at her to pick up her pace. Beth sped up, passed two girls, and moved into second. Carol followed on her heels. Beth knew she had energy now, and she knew what her split time should be, but she decided since she was running amongst such a large group, it would be wiser to save her push until the final lap. Suddenly, Carol pulled up next to her, and slid in front into the first-place position. As they passed by Anne at the halfway point, Beth clearly heard her yelling, "Pick up your pace Beth! This is much too slow for you!" Beth knew the seriousness of her tone. She pulled out and passed Carol. She now held the lead position. She could feel her body adjust to a more demanding pace. Carol pulled up even with Beth and ran alongside of her. It didn't take long before Carol and Beth were significantly in front of the pack. As they passed the coach, Beth saw her check her stopwatch and yell, "Good times! Good times! Try to keep it up!" As they passed Anne, and headed into the final lap, Beth heard Anne yelling at them to push harder. Beth gave it everything she had left. Carol and Beth were still shoulder to shoulder. They were thirty yards ahead of everyone. The other runners lined the side of the track and gathered at the finish line to cheer them on. Beth could barely breathe as she tried to stay even with Carol. She felt her heart pounding, and her legs getting rubbery as they attempted to kick out the final ten yards.

"Wow! Fantastic times girls!" the coach yelled looking at her stopwatch as the two of them crossed the finish line.

"Young lady with the dark hair, I'm sorry I don't know your name yet," she called out to Beth, who was bent over still trying to fill her lungs with air.

The look on Beth's face was one of disappointment and frustration, as she looked up and mumbled between breaths, "Beth Locke...Locke with an E."

"Well...Beth Locke with an E...you were only two seconds behind Carol. That's great!"

"Thank you," she said quietly, then looked at Carol and said with no real sincerity, "Nice run..."

"Thanks Beth, you gave me a run for my money. You're going to be great someday."

"Thank you," is what came out of Beth's mouth, but it wasn't exactly what she was thinking. That would've been too inappropriate to say out loud. She didn't like being patronized, especially by Carol.

"Nice run!" Anne said with excitement as she came over to them, "Your times were as good as last year's top ten division runners. We're going to have a hell of a team this season!"

Beth, still bent over trying to catch her breath, just nodded. Carol, seemingly less exhausted, went over to Anne and put her arm around Anne's shoulder, "We're just trying to keep up with you..." she said with a big grin.

When practice was over, Beth and Anne walked back to the car. Beth barely said a word.

"Are you okay Beth?"

"No...I'm embarrassed she beat me."

"I told you she was a university scholarship runner. She's really, really, good. Just keeping up with her tells you how good you are, and you're just beginning! Beth you will be better than her, I promise…"

"Can you beat her?" Beth asked hoping the answer was a clear yes.

"I don't know…but when you and I run together in the finals, we'll cross that finish line in front of her, shoulder to shoulder. I promise."

"I keep my promises…do you?" Beth said seriously.

"If it's humanly possible, I do too," Anne said as she wrapped her arm around Beth's shoulder and gave her a big smile.

CHAPTER TWELVE

The Samba

After two days of tryouts, Beth, Carol, and Anne, were now official members of the college track team. Beth was one of only a few freshmen runners. She knew she had a lot to learn. She listened closely to coach Ryan's instructions and often asked Anne for advice. Carol frequently offered recommendations that Beth never sought. Even though she respected Carol's talent and experience, she found the suggestions to be condescending. When Carol finished giving her a pointer, Beth usually replied, "Yeah...well maybe I'll try that, thanks." She wouldn't take the advice though, unless Anne agreed it would help. Anne always agreed with Carol and encouraged Beth to trust Carol's insights. Beth said she would try, but her heart wasn't in it. Beth had insights of her own.

Practices were long and hard that week. By the time Beth and Anne showered in the locker room, finished dinner in the cafeteria, and then returned to their rooms to study and complete assignments, they were exhausted and needed sleep. They had almost no time or opportunity for intimacy. Anne's straight roommates were almost always there, and were still trying to find Anne, "a prince charming." Beth's roommate, Chris, had apparently stopped seeing her current boyfriend, and seldom left the room. Beth and Anne tried to find a place to be alone. It had to be a location where they wouldn't feel rushed, or nervous that someone might hear them. It was much more difficult than they could've imagined. They stole quick kisses on the elevator, and passionate ones in any hidden place they could find, but they desperately wanted so much more. Anne often told Beth, "Be patient...our time will come." That time would not be this weekend though. Anne would be leaving for home early Saturday morning for a baby shower, and not returning until Sunday night.

Friday's practice was particularly hard. They ran extra laps and sprints, and then headed to the weight room for their bi-weekly workout.

"I think we need to get together tonight and have a little party," Mia said as she finished her final set of leg extensions.

"I'm in. I need a break from all this work," Abby agreed.

"Count me in too," Carol said as she put her weights back on the rack, then walked over to Beth and placed her hands on Beth's shoulders, "Are you going to join us Beth? Freshman are supposed to bring the beer you know," she teased.

"Sorry Carol, but I'll get carded and I'm not a good liar, so I'll bring the chips and dip instead," Beth said with a fake smile.

"Who's place?" Anne asked.

"We can have it at our apartment," Mia said looking over at Abby, her roommate, making sure it was okay. Abby nodded yes, then added, "Meet at our place at 8:00. Bring who you want, and I'll get in touch with some of the guys on the team. We'll get the beer, and the rest of you can bring the snacks or anything else you want."

After the workout, Anne walked out of the gym with Beth, "How about I pick you up, and we'll go get some snacks for the party?"

"Okay, but I'm still a little uncomfortable because of what happened the last time I drank."

"Don't worry, I'll take better care of you this time," Anne said as she wrapped her arm around Beth's shoulder and gave her a big smile.

Around seven forty-five that evening, Anne headed up to Beth's room to pick her up for the party. She passed Chris along the way.

"Why don't you join us tonight Chris?" Anne asked sincerely.

"Thanks for the invite, but I have work to do. Now, you two girls go have fun tonight and make sure you don't behave," she kidded.

"Well...I've never heard it put that way, but thanks," Anne laughed.

When Beth opened the door, Anne just stood in the doorway and held her gaze. "Damn, you look hot! And I thought you looked sexy in running shorts!"

Beth looked stunning. She was dressed in tight black tapered pants that fell on her hips, and a snug, low cut white blouse that accented her cleavage. You could tell there was not one ounce of fat on her body.

"You are absolutely beautiful," Anne said as she closed the door behind her. As she stood there staring at Beth, a big smile filled her face, "You look like a sexy movie star..."

"So do you...It's too bad we don't have enough time to make our own little movie..." Beth said seductively as she pulled Anne close and kissed her intimately.

116

You could hear the laughter and music already playing when Beth and Anne arrived at the apartment. They knocked and let themselves in. Most of the people were sitting on the floor or couch in the living room, and a few were carrying on conversations in the kitchen.

"Hey guys! Come in and bring those chips with you! We need something salty to go with our beer," Abby called out.

"I'm glad you guys made it," Carol said as she got off the couch and walked over to greet them. Beth noticed how attractive Carol looked.

She gave Anne a hug and a kiss on the cheek, then she turned towards Beth and greeted her the same way. It felt fake.

Beth looked around and realized that she was one of the few freshmen. She was comforted by the fact that she knew most of the people there from the track team. There were only a few people that she didn't recognize.

Beth and Anne made their way through a small group of people as they headed to the kitchen. It seemed everyone they passed, wanted to talk to Anne or give her a hug.

"Boy…you have your own little following. Do you give out autographs? Because if you do, I would like to get one," Beth kidded.

"I'd like to give you more than an autograph…" Anne replied softly with a wink.

The night was full of laughter, storytelling, drinking, and flirting. About an hour into the party, a few people started dancing. Some of the dancers were particularly good, others couldn't follow the beat, but no one cared. Anne proved to be an excellent dancer, and as much as Beth didn't want to admit it, so was Carol. It seemed normal for girls to dance together, but the same did not stand true for the guys. Anne and Carol danced together for several songs, but not to any slow songs. Beth had chosen not to dance, up to this point.

A very handsome upperclassman, who appeared to be part Hispanic, approached Beth, and whispered to her, "Why do I feel like you know how to Samba?" A big smile came over Beth's face that she couldn't hide. "How did you know?"

"Oh…pretty lady, I can tell we share a culture that practically owns that dance. I bet you learned it before you learned to ride a bike."

"I was in fourth grade when my Grandmother first taught me," Beth said laughing.

"I think I was still in diapers. It's like we have a secret cult. One samba dancer can always pick out another. Are you Brazilian?"

"I'm a little bit of everything, but if you could ask my grandmother, she would tell you the only one that counts are my Brazilian roots. She taught my mother when she was very young, and made sure my Italian father learned it, so he could dance it at their wedding. When I was young, my whole family would put on Samba music and dance in the living room. Watching my father move his hips was hysterical, but he was always a good sport."

"It's such a sexy dance if you do it right," he said playfully.

"Not when you're dancing with your older brother."

"Ahhh…then it's time to dance with a handsome stranger," he said with a suggestive grin.

"If you think I would dance in front of everyone, you're crazy."

"I have an idea. I will teach everyone the basics. You will be my assistant. Then we'll show them how it should really be done. You're so beautiful and sexy…we'll make the perfect Samba partners."

"I'll admit, I would love to dance again, but not here."

"Well, at least help me teach them. Please…" His sweet white smile stood out against his brown hair and dark brown puppy dog eyes. Beth had just enough alcohol in her to reluctantly agree.

"May I have everyone's attention please?" he called out confidently. Someone turned down the music so he could be heard.

"For those few in here who don't know me already, my name is Marco Dias. My lovely and talented friend Beth and I, are going to teach you the most famous dance of our heritage…THE SAMBA!" Beth thought she was going to die. Before she had a chance to say no, everyone herded into the living room to take advantage of the free lesson, or at least watch. Some were cheering and encouraging others to join in. Anne and Carol seemed to be the most enthusiastic. Marco put on "Sonho Meu," a famous song often used for dancing the Samba. Beth knew that song well. It reminded her of her family. She felt reminiscent and remembered the joy and laughter she felt when they played that song. She wanted to dance.

Marco was a great instructor. He had them moving their hips and arms to create a modified version of this energetic, yet sultry dance. Beth enjoyed helping the crowd of happy dancers, who were sometimes laughing so hard they had to stop. Beth didn't work with Anne or Carol, but it wasn't intentional. Marco took an interest in them right away.

After 20 minutes of trying to help the eager participants, Marco called out, "Please clear the dance floor. My gorgeous and irresistible partner and I will show you how this dance is properly done. Music please," He grabbed Beth and took her to the center of the living room. She felt like she was in a trance. Suddenly the music came on. Marco placed his hand on her hip and pulled her into the rhythm of the music. Happy flashbacks and lucid memories of the dance moves that she had practiced a thousand times, guided her through this passionate dance. The Samba was filled with suggestive hip action, and sexy graceful body movements. Marco was brilliant and complimented her moves with perfectly choreographed steps. Her classmates went wild. They cheered and whistled. Beth was oblivious. When the music stopped, the enthusiastic applause began. It was at this point that Beth's face flushed red with embarrassment. Anne came over and hugged her. "Oh my God, Beth! You were fantastic! I had no idea you could dance like that!" Then she whispered in her ear, "You were so sexy, I can't stand it."

"I think I just completely embarrassed myself," Beth winced.

"No! You were amazing! Damn Beth...you're hot!" Anne couldn't stop smiling. Then she said so no one could hear, "I can't wait to have a private dance, so I can put my hands on those sexy little hips."

Marco approached Beth, "Ahhh…Meu parceiro gostosa de danca, I will be seeing you again," then he kissed her on both cheeks and walked away.

For the next hour, Beth sat on the couch with Anne and Carol. They shared their thoughts and told stories, usually about track. Beth could tell Carol was getting drunk, but by no means was she out of control. Beth learned that track ran in Carol's family, and both of her parents and one brother, were accomplished college athletes. She also learned that Carol's family were very well to do. Just like Anne.

Beth mingled with classmates on her way to the kitchen. Most of them wanted to know how she learned to dance the Samba. She was relaxed and enjoying the party. After ten minutes in the kitchen, she returned and saw that Anne and Carol were no longer seated on the couch. Two other girls had taken their places. She decided this was as good a time as any to go to the bathroom. She didn't want to use the one downstairs because there was a line, and she knew from being in the apartment before, there was one by Mia's room upstairs. She climbed the steps and turned the corner. She saw Anne and Carol standing at the other end of the hallway.

She watched, unnoticed, as Carol took Anne's face in her hands and kissed her on the lips. She heard Carol say, "That's something I miss very much." Beth's heart stopped. She turned and hurried down the steps.

Beth said nothing about what she had witnessed for the rest of the evening, largely because she was trying not to cry. She was well practiced at hiding her hurt.

As Beth and Anne were leaving the party, Marco called out across the room trying to get Beth's attention, "Beth, minha linda dancarina, wait I need to ask you… Voce tem um namorado? Voce tem namorada?",

"Nao tenho certeza," she answered with barely a smile.

"What did he say?" Anne asked quickly.

"He called me his beautiful little dancer, and he wanted to know if I had a boyfriend or a girlfriend."

"What did you tell him?"

"I told him I'm not sure I have either." After what she witnessed tonight, it was the truth.

As they pulled up to the dorm, Anne said, "I'm so sorry I'm not going to be around this weekend. If I could get out of going to my cousin's baby shower, believe me I would. I miss you already, but I'll try to call. You owe me a dance," Anne said with a suggestive grin, then she looked around to see if anyone was watching and leaned over to give Beth a long soft kiss. "Thanks for going with me tonight, I had a good time."

Beth just smiled, "I know you did …"

"I really love you Beth. Please make sure you have some fun this weekend. Give the running and studying a break. Do something different!" she laughed.

"Okay Anne. I hear you. Maybe I will try to do something different this weekend…"

CHAPTER THIRTEEN

Date with Marco

It was around eleven o'clock in the morning and Beth had just gotten back from her run when the phone rang.

"Ola minha dancarina de samba sexy…this is Marco," he said with an intentionally strong accent.

"I'm not your sexy dancer, but thanks for the compliment. What are you doing calling me? Didn't you torture me enough already?" she kidded but enjoyed his flattery.

"I can't stop thinking about you. You filled my heart with joy last night."

"Stop the corny stuff Marco, what do you want?"

"Okay, okay," Marco said without his accent. "I really did have a lot of fun last night, and I'm not kidding, you really are a sexy dancer!"

"I don't know about the sexy dancer part, but I have to admit, I had fun too. It's been so long since I've had the chance to dance, that I forgot how much I enjoyed it." Beth felt very comfortable talking to Marco. Maybe it was because they shared a heritage that others knew little about.

"You never told me if you had a boyfriend or a girlfriend last night, so I'm taking a chance to see if you're open to going out with me. We don't have to call it a date. I just want to spend some time with you. I feel like I can be myself with you, and I think you know you can always be yourself around me. I feel like I know you somehow. It's like we're already friends, but not because we're on the same track team. You probably didn't even notice me anyway. Maybe we knew each other when we were little!"

"Maybe you're my half-brother!" Beth teased.

"Oh no…don't say that! That wouldn't work for me."

"You better not get any big ideas Marco," Beth warned.

"So, what time can I pick you up?"

"Well, what are we going to do?"

"Dinner and a movie. How about I just come to your room around 5:00 and we can figure out the details?"

"Okay, don't be late. I have to get back by midnight or I'll turn into a pumpkin."

"See you soon minha dancarina sexy." Beth liked Marco. She was more comfortable around him than she was with most guys. She was looking forward to tonight. She thought it would be a good distraction from the emotional anguish that consumed her. It simply crushed her to see Anne and Carol kissing. She knew Anne loved her and couldn't understand why she was kissing someone else, especially Carol. Perhaps, Beth thought, Anne wasn't over Carol. Or maybe Anne thought seeing others was an acceptable part of their relationship. They never really talked about it.

Marco would be picking Beth up in a half hour. She decided she might need a jacket to go with what she was wearing. She went next door to borrow one. The door was ajar, so she stuck her head in the door and asked, "Hey Barb, do you have a dress up jacket I can borrow? Most of mine are running jackets."

Barb was sitting at her desk. "Sure Beth. What's the occasion?"

"I'm going out with some guy this evening."

"Oh my…big date huh? Who's the lucky fella?" Barb asked as she got up and opened her closet.

"Marco Diaz. I met him at a party, he's on my track team," Beth said as she chose the jacket she wanted to borrow.

"Oh my God! I know who he is. He's gorgeous! Do you know how many women would love to be in your shoes? Here, let me give you a little something," she said as she pulled something out of her desk drawer. "Here take this," she said as she slipped it in the jacket pocket.

"What is it?

"Oh Lord…just take it and get out of here so I can study," she kidded.

Marco was right on time. "Ola minha dancarina sexy," he said as he bent forward and bowed.

"Ola meu lindo principe," she said and returned his bow.

"Wow…I'm already your handsome prince and we haven't even gone out yet," he teased. Then he added with mild urgency, "Let's go, I'm doubled parked." Beth's heart skipped a beat. Anne had said the same exact thing when they were leaving for her parent's house. It took Beth a concerted effort to shake it off. She was determined to enjoy her evening.

As they walked out of the dorm, Marco reached for Beth's hand to hold. Beth pulled her hand back and kidded, "Really Marco? I thought this wasn't a date."

"You can't kill a guy for trying," he said grinning.

Marco took Beth to an upscale restaurant. Beth hadn't expected that, but she had dressed appropriately, just in case. They looked like the perfect young couple. One gorgeous, one handsome, and both with bodies that people envied. Beth could sense people staring at them. It made her a bit uncomfortable. She didn't like being the center of attention, as she sensed Marco did.

Beth told Marco she loved her dinner. She had Chicken Caesar Salad and a sweet potato, as a side dish. Marco thought she should have ordered a full entrée, but Beth rebutted with a big smile, "You told me to be myself, and that's what I would have gotten if I was out with my friends." When she said "friends", she pictured only Anne.

Beth was enjoying the evening. Discussion came easy. Topics included, Brazil, dancing, track, and what he had planned for the rest of the evening. His intention was to take her to an old drive-in movie theater that only showed older popular movies. The movie *Rocky* was playing tonight. Beth thought that was a great idea. She loved that movie and told Marco it might inspire them to work out harder.

Marco pulled his van into the back row of the drive-in movie's parking area. They arrived at eight o'clock for the nine o'clock movie.

"Come in the back of the van with me so I can show you some of the cool stuff I put in. It was an empty container when I bought it. I designed everything and installed it myself.

"Very impressive," Beth said sincerely.

"Here sit down," he said pointing to a little couch. He reached into a small refrigerator and pulled out a bottle of wine. Then he grabbed two plastic cups off the counter. "I just want you to try this. It's very sweet and doesn't have a high alcohol content. I promise you'll like it." Beth took a swallow and found she actually did like it. They talked for about a half hour as they finished off the bottle.

"I know you probably don't smoke, but I'm wondering if you're feeling daring enough tonight to try a little pot. It's not the strong stuff. It will just make you feel a little mellow." Beth just stared at him. He continued as if he felt he still had a chance to convince her.

"You must think I'm wild because I'm drinking wine and smoking, but I honestly only do this quite sparingly. I swear. I take my running too seriously to mess up my body. Even most doctors say if you just do it occasionally, it doesn't seem to do any harm." Beth recalled what Anne had said about trying something different. She was nervous about smoking but gave him an answer before she could talk herself out of it, "Okay, I'll try it, but don't let me get too high." Marco lit the joint and took a drag. He handed it to Beth with the instructions, "Don't take a deep drag until you get used to it, otherwise you will start coughing and gagging on it." Beth took a little drag and swallowed the smoke, trying not to look too amateurish. She handed the joint back, "Yuck, this tastes terrible!"

"I know, but wait a little while, you'll start feeling really mellow." They finished the joint and passed the time talking about their favorite movies.

"I think I'm high," Beth giggled. Marco looked at her eyes and laughed, "I think you are too."

"Oh shit...does it get worse?

"No, it gets better," Marco said as he leaned over and kissed her on the lips. He kept his face close after he took his lips off hers and whispered, "You are beautiful. Those gorgeous brown eyes of yours drive me crazy.

They're even beautiful when they're red." Beth just smiled. She was enjoying the high. Marco took her hands and pulled her up out of her seat.

"Let me show you something." Marco pulled the couch out and it transformed into a bed. The back rest acted as a mattress, that now was laying on a platform.

"Pretty creative, huh," he said proudly.

"Oh my God Marco...only you would think of something like that," she laughed as she gave him a gentle slap on his shoulder. She was starting to feel happy, even giddy and was not fighting it off.

"It's getting hot in here," he said as he pulled off his jacket. Here, let me take your jacket." Marco helped Beth pull off her borrowed jacket. Instead of putting it down, he slipped it on. "Does it do me justice?" he said as he put his hands in the pockets and spun around like a model. Beth started laughing. He looked awfully cute. His long arms were hanging out of the short sleeves, and he made a different face with each pose he made.

"You look adorable," Beth said then grabbed his jacket and put it on. "May I have this dance?" she asked.

"Why certainly," he said as he tried to find Beth's hands hidden in the long sleeves of his jacket.

"Samba?" he asked as he put his hands out invitingly. Beth nodded yes, took his hands, and began trying to dance in the back of the van, to whatever Samba music Marco was humming or singing. He couldn't raise his arms above his waist, or he would rip the jacket. Beth couldn't stop laughing. She understood now why so many people enjoy getting high. Finally, she stopped long enough to announce, "I think I've got the munchies. That's what they call it, isn't it?" Marco chuckled as he went to a cabinet and tried to pull out a box of Cheerios without ripping the jacket. "Here, this is the best I can offer you." Beth started laughing again as she took the box and opened it. They each took turns reaching in and taking out handfuls of cereal.

"Had enough?" he teased. Beth just laughed. He took the box out of Beth's hand and returned it to the cabinet, then came back and put his arms around her waist. His voice got more serious, "Let's get these jackets off and sit down." Beth followed his lead and took off her jacket and sat down on the bed. Marco took her hands and began to gaze into her eyes. She began to feel a little uncomfortable but was mellow enough to ignore it.

"Why are you staring? Say something," Beth said smiling.

"No, I don't think I want to talk anymore," he said in a soft voice, then he placed his hands against her shoulders and pushed her gently back onto the bed. He began kissing her. Soon his lips parted, and his tongue slipped into her mouth. Beth tried to enjoy it. She attempted to convince herself to give him time, her body would respond soon. Girls were supposed to enjoy being kissed by a gorgeous guy like Marco. She was determined to enjoy it. Besides, Anne had encouraged her to do something different, and this wasn't cheating, because Anne had already established those rules. She felt his hands slide up her sides. His hands moved slowly towards her breasts, then Beth felt one of his thumbs rub across her bra. She let him do it because she thought it might feel as good as when Anne touched her. It didn't. She kept telling herself to relax and enjoy it. He sat up and slowly unbuttoned her blouse and helped her take it off.

"You have a perfect body," he whispered, then unbuttoned his own shirt and pulled it off. He was slim and very muscular. His pants sat low and Beth could see a little hair below his muscular abdomen. Beth found it sexy but was growing a little uneasy. She kept telling herself that almost all college women had gone further than she had. She didn't want to be left out. She didn't want to be a virgin anymore. She knew that Anne had plenty of sex with her boyfriends, so why shouldn't she. Marco didn't stop with his shirt. After he slipped out of his loafers, he unzipped his pants and took them off. Beth just laid there. He stood over her and she could see that his boxers were starting to show his excitement. Marco lowered himself on top of her. She could feel the hair on his chest on her skin. He began kissing her again but this time with more pressure. She put her arms around him, and French kissed him. It didn't feel right. It was nothing like when she kissed Anne. There was no excitement, no emotion. Very simply, there was no love. Marco reached behind Beth and unhooked her bra with one hand. Beth felt him getting hard between her legs. She began to panic. Marco slid his hand under her loose bra and ran his fingers across her breasts. He moved his head down so he could place his mouth on them and use his tongue. Beth closed her eyes tightly. It didn't feel good, it just wasn't right. Marco reached down with one hand and unbuttoned her slacks then began to slide his hand down under her bikini panties. It didn't feel good…something was missing.

"Stop Marco…," Beth said quietly as she grabbed his hand.

"What's the matter?" he asked confused.

"I just can't do this. This isn't right for me." Marco just stared at her.

"Oh, come on Beth…what's wrong?"

"I'm sorry…I can't explain it. It just doesn't feel right."

"Don't you like me?"

"Yes, I like you. I guess I just have to love you, and I don't."

"Then why did you bring a condom?"

Beth's eyes opened wide. "What condom?"

"I found it in your jacket pocket." It suddenly occurred to Beth what Brenda had slipped into her pocket. She had forgotten all about it. "It's not my jacket. I borrowed it. I didn't know." Marco just looked at Beth. She couldn't tell if he believed her or not. Marco pushed himself away from her and stood up. He didn't say anything as he began to put his clothes back on. Beth stood up, zipped up her pants and put her bra and shirt back on. Marco sat down on the bed and patted the spot next to him. "Here, sit down." Beth complied.

"If this was any other girl besides you Beth, I would call you a tease."

"Marco you promised I could completely be myself with you. Well, I am. I'm still a virgin Marco. I've never had intercourse, and I know I just don't want to do this," Beth said assertively.

Marco just looked at her while he was thinking, then agreed, "If it's not right for you…then I'm glad you were honest with me. BUT…if you ever change your mind, I want to be your first," he said as he gave her a soft kiss on the cheek. He stared at her for a moment then admitted, "I've got to tell you Beth… you're absolutely adorable, and you're not even aware of it. I'm totally attracted to you…" he said as he shook his head and added, "I can see why Anne is too."

"What?"

"I saw how she looked at you at the party. She couldn't have hidden it even if she wanted to." Beth laughed and said, "You're crazy Marco."

"Ahhh…I know true love when I see it," he said with a sweet, perceptive grin.

It was a quiet ride home.

CHAPTER FOURTEEN

Three Not So Great Days…

Sunday

Anne called Beth Sunday morning before Beth went out for her run. They didn't talk long, but long enough for Anne to describe how boring the baby shower was, and that she was going to spend the rest of the day with her family. She told Beth she missed her and couldn't wait to see her at practice on Monday. Beth didn't share what happened on Saturday night with Marco, except to say she watched "Rocky."

Beth went to the library Sunday night to have some private time to think, and if she could, study.

Anne got back from her parent's house earlier than she expected. She went over to Beth's dorm to surprise her. When she knocked on the door, Chris answered, "Oh hi Anne!"

"Is Beth around?"

"No. She's not. I think she's over at the library. Hey, did you hear about her date? She went out with Marco Diaz! He's gorgeous, and from what I hear from other girls, he's a real man, if you know what I mean."

"You mean the Marco who's on our track team?" Anne asked, the smile leaving her face. She looked upset but Chris didn't seem to notice.

"I think that's what she said, but you know Beth, she's not talking. I think she likes to keep all the juicy details to herself, that little rat." Anne forced out a quiet laugh and said, "Yeah well that's Beth. I think she likes being mysterious. If she comes back, don't tell her I was here. I want to keep it a surprise."

"Sure thing...will do."

Monday

Monday afternoon came quickly, and Beth was already stretching out by the track when she saw Anne heading towards her. She felt her heart beat harder. She walked up to greet Anne and gave her a hug. Anne squeezed her extra tight and whispered, "I love you Beth."

"I love you too," Beth whispered back. She wasn't lying...but she felt guilty because her thoughts and feelings were still scrambled. She couldn't stop envisioning Carol kissing Beth or Carlos kissing her. She felt lost. Practice was going to be hard today. Tomorrow would be easier because they needed to rest for their first meet on Wednesday.

Beth finished stretching and was standing by the edge of the track when coach Ryan approached her and put her arm around her shoulder. "Beth..." she said with a kind smile, "I want to tell you how impressed I am with your work ethic. You and Anne are some of the most dedicated runners I've been lucky enough to coach. I'm quite aware and very impressed that you both put in a lot of extra time after practice and on weekends. I think Anne's the best mentor you'll ever have. She is truly one of a kind...but you're full of raw talent and you're only going to get better. I just wanted to let you know, it's okay for you to beat Anne occasionally. I know Anne, she won't mind. She just wants you to be the best that you can be." She squeezed Beth's shoulder, gave her a couple pats on the back, and walked away. She didn't give Beth any time to respond.

Anne wasn't her usual jovial self during the warm-ups. Beth took note that Anne was much quieter and didn't engage with anyone. This was totally out of character. Beth hoped it was because Anne was racked with guilt, because of the kiss with Carol. As soon as practice began, Beth and Anne had little time to talk to each other. Coach Ryan was working one on one with Beth, and Anne was working exclusively with Carol on mile pacing. Beth tried to concentrate on the instructions Coach Ryan was giving her, but she kept seeing Anne and Carol flying by, running shoulder to shoulder. Maybe Carol wasn't actually smiling at her, but Beth felt like she was. After practice ended, they showered and went over to the cafeteria for a quick dinner. The table was full of talkative track team members, and it was easy for Beth to avoid talking to Anne. Anne didn't say much at dinner anyway. She seemed distracted.

Beth and Anne exited the cafeteria and started to walk back to Beth's dorm, where Anne's car was parked. They walked without talking. When they were about halfway there, Anne pulled Beth behind a large tree and kissed her softly. Then she stepped back and looked into Beth's eyes. Beth kept Anne's eye contact, but couldn't say anything except, "I'll see you tomorrow." Beth was too overwhelmed with anger, hurt, guilt, and love. Her strongest emotion, however, was by far her indisputable love. Anne continued to look at Beth as though she was waiting for her to say something else, but Beth remained quiet. Finally, Anne said somberly, "Okay…I'll see you tomorrow," then gave her one more soft kiss. The moment felt awkward.

Tuesday

With the opening meet tomorrow, today's practice wasn't going to be full out. At the beginning of practice, Anne told Beth that she would be leaving a little early because she had a supervisory meeting with other pre-med students. During practice, Anne, Beth, and Carol, were given instructions to run their mile at a three-quarter pace.

Beth made sure she was standing right next to Anne when they took off. All three stayed even for the first lap, but Beth picked up the pace going into the second lap, and the other two stayed with her. Carol pulled out ahead of Beth and Anne, with a quarter mile left. Beth's adrenalin kicked in, and she passed Carol to put herself in the lead. The pace was becoming full out, not the three-quarter pace they were instructed to do. As they sprinted across the finish line, Carol and Beth were shoulder to shoulder, but Anne was one step in front of them. All three slowed down and tried to catch their breath.

Anne came over to Carol and Beth, who were near each other, but not next to each other. "What the hell was that?" she said angrily.

"That pace was too slow. I wasn't getting enough of a workout." Beth said, still trying to catch her breath.

Anne was mad, "We weren't supposed to! We're a team, remember? We stick together! We don't need to make bad choices that we may regret!" She said no more. She grabbed her bag and left. Carol said nothing and wouldn't look at Beth. Beth just stood there and watched Anne walk away.

After practice was over, Beth walked back to the locker room. It was crowded with women athletes from a variety of teams, who had also just finished their practices. The rows of lockers buzzed with liveliness. Everyone seemed to be laughing or talking about their coaches, teammates, games, boyfriends, or classes. Except Beth, who stood alone, quietly listening to the noise around her. She was ashamed of her behavior and miserable that she had disappointed Anne. They needed to talk, and she knew she couldn't wait any longer. Suddenly she heard a familiar voice in the next aisle over. It was Carol. "I'm glad I'm done for the day. I couldn't wait for practice to be over. I'm not sure how much I like running track anymore," she said sounding frustrated.

"You're just saying that because you're not number one anymore, like you were in your old college. Anne and that new freshmen are taking away all your glory," an unfamiliar voice teased. Another voice that Beth didn't recognize jumped in.

"Are those the two that run together the whole way and finish side by side? I heard about them. The Siamese queers," she said trying to be funny. Beth froze, her body couldn't move, her heart sank. She couldn't believe what she had just heard. How could anyone say something like that? She heard a few girls laughing. Then a strong voice spoke up. It was Carol. "Shut up Lisa! You don't even know them. You're fucking rude. Why don't you mind your own business and grow up?" Beth was still in shock as she walked down her aisle, then turned and faced the group of girls she had just overheard. She stood there expressionless. Neither Lisa nor Carol had looked up yet, but the others did and became silent.

"If you're calling me a queer because I love Ann, then I guess I am," Beth said as she walked slowly towards the group. "But I'm not ashamed of loving her. Our closeness is a blessing that most people can only dream of. She has done more for me than anyone ever has. She has done a lot for everyone on our team. Especially you Carol." Then Beth stopped directly in front of Lisa, and looked into her eyes, "By the way…Carol was right...mind your own fucking business and grow up."

Beth was still shaking as she walked back to her locker.

"I'm sorry you had to hear that Beth. That girl's just an immature jerk that needs attention," Carol said apologetically as she approached Beth.

"You didn't have to stand up for me, I can handle this myself you know." Carol just looked at Beth for a moment before she spoke, "I wasn't standing up for you. I was standing up for Anne."

"Why? Because you're still in love with her?"

"Yes, I am. I can't help it. You of all people should understand why."

"Well, she must love you too…I saw you kiss at the party."

Carol paused for a moment and stared at Beth, "Oh really…then I guess you didn't watch long enough." Beth didn't say anything. Carol took the sarcasm out of her tone, and said with sincerity, "Beth, I know Anne will always love me, but it's not the same way she loves you. You better realize that before it's too late. You two need to talk."

CHAPTER FIFTEEN

"I Need to Tell You Something"

Back at the dorm, Beth waited until she thought Anne was home from her meeting and then called. "Hi Anne," Beth said quietly.

"Hey Beth," Anne replied indifferently. Beth could tell she was still mad at her.

"I'm sorry about this afternoon. I know I acted like a real asshole."

She could hear Anne chuckle quietly on the other end. She pictured Anne trying not to smile.

"You were an asshole. What the hell was that all about?" she asked, still sounding frustrated.

"Can we talk? Maybe face to face so I don't have to explain over the phone."

"Yeah...I think that would be a good idea. We obviously have some important things to talk about. How about I pick you up and bring you back here? I found out my roommates are going to be gone for a couple of days." Beth loved the idea of having complete privacy.

"I'll leave in five minutes, meet me out front."

Beth waited nervously, trying to figure out how to handle this. She'd been going over in her head exactly what she'd say, and the tone of voice she'd use. She was still unsure if she should tell her about what happened in the locker room.

Anne's car pulled up. "How did your meeting go?" Beth said when she got into the car. It was her planned ice breaker. Anne leaned over, looked into Beth's eyes, and gave her a gentle kiss.

"I've missed you," Anne said softly. That kiss did Beth in. She became lost in her emotions and could no longer follow her carefully designed script. She let her guilt

146

pour out, "I'm so sorry Anne…I got carried away. I just wanted to beat her."

"Why? What the hell did you need to prove, and who did you think you needed to prove it to?" Her voice didn't hide her frustration and confusion.

Beth's voice started to crack, "I needed to prove to you that I'm better than her!" Anne looked at Beth, pulled off to the side of the road and shut the car off. Beth waited until Anne looked at her, then blurted out, "Anne…I saw you kiss her at the party!" Anne said nothing as she focused on Beth's eyes. Beth couldn't hide her anxiety as she waited for Anne to explain. She hoped what Carol had implied was true.

"I didn't kiss her Beth…she kissed me."

"Is there really a difference?"

"Yes of course. She didn't know you and I were together. She apologized to me after I told her about us. I told her I was committed to you, and it wasn't going to change."

"I heard her tell you that she missed kissing you. Do you feel the same?"

"Beth," Anne paused, then took Beth's hands and spoke softly, "I treasure my memories of being with people that I cared about. It doesn't matter if it's a guy or girl. Those memories, and the feelings they stir up, belong to me and are a part of me. It's nothing to be jealous of. I would love to know that your life has been filled with love and excitement, and that you still carry those happy memories with you. It wouldn't change how much I love you. How could it?" Beth had no answer. Instead, she said calmly,

"She still loves you, you know?"

"I know, she told me. I told her I love her too, but it's a different kind of love. She knows how I feel. We've always been honest with each other. She knows I won't leave you." Beth sat silently and looked at Anne. She trusted Anne and was ashamed that she had questioned her behavior.

"I'm sorry Anne. I've never been jealous before. I swear. I didn't even realize I was. I'm such a beginner at this type of relationship. I started to believe that maybe being gay, meant that it was okay to see other people." Anne shook her head, "Maybe it's okay for some people, but it's not okay with me." Beth's expression changed to dread when she realized she would have to tell Anne about her date with Marco.

"Anne, I have to tell you something…I went out with someone Saturday night. His name is Marco and—"

"Stop," Anne interrupted her, "I already know."

"How did you find out?" Beth said surprised.

"Chris told me."

"When?"

"Sunday night. I got back early, so I went over to your room to surprise you, but I guess I'm the one that got the biggest surprise."

"I'm sorry. I can explain my thinking then, but it might not make sense now."

"Let's just hold off on that for now. I want to get off the side of the road and go to my apartment, where we'll be alone."

Anne unlocked her apartment door and told Beth to come in and make herself comfortable on the couch.

"What can I get you? You know I don't cook much, but I do have some snacks."

"Do you have any chocolate?" Beth answered chuckling.

"Yeah…I think I have some little Kit Kats in the fridge, I only like them if they're cold."

"Me too! They're my favorite! See how much we have in common."

"What do you want to drink?"

"Do you have any diet soda? If you do, we could split it. I don't want to be up all night."

"Hmmm…I hope you're wrong about that," Anne mumbled as she walked away.

After they got settled on the couch, Anne finally asked Beth for an explanation.

"Beth, please tell me why you went out with Marco? I don't get it. You never mentioned you were even thinking about something like that."

"I know…I'm sorry. It seems crazy now, but it didn't then. Remember, I saw you and Carol kiss! I thought you had started to see her but didn't tell me. I didn't want to believe you were cheating, so I guess my brain just convinced me it was okay to see other people."

"Okay I'll give you that, but you should have asked."

"You should have told me. I shouldn't have needed to ask." Anne didn't say anything for a moment, then said, "I'm sorry, I should've. I guess I didn't want to upset you."

"There's another reason I went out with Marco…" Anne watched and waited for Beth to continue. "Oh boy…I almost hate to admit this, but I've never gone all the way

149

with a guy before. I barely made it to third base." Anne laughed, and Beth added,

"You have to agree that Marco is gorgeous. I thought he might just be the one to do it with."

"Beth! What were you thinking?"

"Well…you have done it plenty of times, so I thought it must be good," Beth said almost laughing. Anne quickly interjected, "I didn't have that much sex!"

"Anyway…I guess I wanted to feel whatever you felt when you were with a guy. I tried to relax and enjoy it, but I couldn't. I didn't like him kissing me. His face was bristly, not soft, and smooth like yours. When he started touching me—" Beth never got to finish, Anne stopped her. "Okay I get it."

"Well, you wanted to know," Beth reminded her. "I have to tell you Anne…it's not the same as when you kiss and touch me. It's completely different, I never even got excited," then she grinned and added, "and I should have because I smoked a joint and I was really high."

"What the hell! I can't believe this!" Anne had to laugh, "I leave you for two days and you turn into a sex fiend drug addict?" They shared their laughter.

"No, really Anne," Beth got serious, "What did it feel like when you made love to your boyfriends?"

"It's not easy to explain…I guess it was mostly just physical. There was some emotion, but it's nothing like I feel when I'm with you. There's just no comparison. With you, it's like this tremendous chemical reaction. Every part of my mind and body is drawn to you," she said as she started to inch closer to Beth, "I just can't get close enough…I want to feel every part of you," Anne said quietly, then leaned towards Beth with a suggestive grin and kissed her. "You have the softest lips I've ever kissed," she said quietly. "I take that as a big compliment considering the size of your sample pool," Beth joked. Anne kissed her gently on her neck. Beth's body was responding.

"I think it's time for a pajama party," Anne whispered in Beth's ear.

"I don't have any pajamas with me, just the sweatpants and top I have on," Beth teased.

"That's okay...you're not going to need them," Anne said as she took Beth's hands, and pulled her up from the couch.

"You do know we have a meet tomorrow?" Beth said as she followed Anne into the bedroom.

"Yeah...consider this our warm-up."

CHAPTER SIXTEEN

Pajama Party

153

The light in the bedroom was dim, but just bright enough for Beth to look into Anne's beautiful clear blue eyes. Anne took Beth's hands and led her to the side of the bed.

"I've been waiting for this for a long time," Anne said softly and kissed Beth's lips so delicately that Beth felt cheated.

"Let's get into our pajamas," Anne said grinning as she slowly unzipped Beth's top, and helped pull her arms out of the sleeves. Beth's body was perfect. Her stomach was muscular and flat, but her breasts were full.

Anne gave Beth a sexually inviting smile, as she began to unbutton her own blouse. After one button, she smiled and said seductively, "You can take care of the rest…"

Beth slowly unbuttoned Anne's blouse, revealing more of Anne's beautiful figure with each button. Beth continued towards the snap on Anne's jeans, but Anne reached for Beth's hands and stopped her. Without releasing her hands, she used them to unhurriedly guide Beth down onto her bed until Beth's body was stretched out and her head lay on a soft pillow. Anne said nothing as she leaned over and began placing soft kisses down Beth's body. When she reached Beth's sweatpants, she untied the bow and slowly slid Beth's pants off, exposing her legs and black briefs. Anne continued to undress Beth, "Sit up and let me help you get that bra off," Anne whispered. Beth sat up and raised her arms in the air so Anne could pull the bra over her breasts and head. Anne carefully removed it and deliberately let it drop from her hands onto the floor.

"You are drop dead gorgeous…" Anne said shaking her head as she stared at Beth's body.

Beth's eyes were fixed on Anne. Anne's white blouse was open, and Beth could see the white lace bra beneath it. Anne's tan, and her low cut jeans helped display how slim and defined her figure was. Beth's heart was pounding.

"You have no idea how sexy you look right now, and how much I want you," Beth said softly with a big grin on her face. Beth's deep love for Anne was magnifying her excitement. She desperately wanted to hold and touch Anne. Beth pulled Anne close and tenderly kissed the skin above her jeans. She could almost taste the sweetness. Beth craved more.

"Now I need to see what your pajamas look like…" Beth said teasingly as a little smile spread across her face. She stood and slowly began to undress Anne. Beth's excitement grew as each piece of clothing came off, particularly the lace bra. Almost all of Anne's clothing now laid on the floor. Before Beth took off Anne's white lace panties, she told Anne to lay down on the bed, then Beth gently lowered herself on top of her. Beth rested her weight on her elbows, but she could feel Anne's warm body beneath her. They exchanged passionate kisses and Beth's desire grew stronger. Anne reached for Beth's hips and grasped her underwear. She pushed them down as far as she could, as though she were sending Beth a clear message to take them off. Beth stood up and removed them. Then she hastily reached for Anne's. Anne lifted her hips to help. Beth pulled them down Anne's long legs and threw them on the floor where they landed on top of the other already removed clothing. Beth laid herself back down so she could place tender kisses on Anne's neck and smell the sweet scent of Anne's familiar perfume. Beth's lips slowly made their way to Anne's soft breasts.

"Oh my God Beth...you're killing me," Anne sighed as Beth continued to arouse her. Anne's breathing grew faster and deeper as she ran her fingers through Beth's hair. Anne seemed as though she might surrender to the stimulation, but instead, pulled Beth's lips back to hers, and gave her impassioned kisses.

"Let's finish what we started in the pond..." Anne said as she turned Beth onto her back and placed her warm, pink lips on Beth's breast. Beth felt Anne's tongue delicately touch her nipples. Slowly and deliberately, Anne began to slide her hand down Beth's naked body. Beth's breathing grew deeper and faster from the excitement of anticipation. Soon she felt Anne touching the warmth and wetness of her body. Anne was finding the exact places that intensified the sensation of her passion. Her body was no longer hers, and she had no power to control what it craved to do. Each touch, each gentle motion she sensed, escalated her arousal.

"Oh my God Anne, please don't stop," she whispered as she leaned her head back and closed her eyes. The stimulation was fully satisfying her. She reached the peak of her excitement and lost herself in the euphoria, "Oh God Anne...", she moaned loudly as her back arched and her body climaxed into a series of powerful and exhilarating contractions. Anne quickly repositioned herself, and placed tender kisses on Beth's lips, as Beth's body trembled. Beth reached for Anne's face and whispered, "Oh my God Anne...I love you so much. You'll never know what you do to me..." Beth felt weak.

She was overcome with emotional and physical fulfilment. She couldn't separate the two. She didn't want to. Anne wrapped her arm over Beth and held her tightly. Beth allowed the security of Anne's embrace to comfort her for a couple of minutes before she spoke. "I'm sorry...I just had to rest for a moment. You wiped me out," she laughed quietly. They smiled at each other. Beth took one hand and moved a strand of blonde hair away from Anne's eyes. "You're gorgeous...I can't believe how lucky I am. Do you know how many people would love to be here with you?"

Anne kissed her gently and said softly, "There's no one in the world that I would rather be lying next to. I don't think I could love you any deeper." Beth turned on her side and gazed into Anne's eyes. She lifted her hand and gently placed it on Anne's hip, then slowly began to descend the contours of Anne's tempting body, as she whispered, "This pajama party isn't over yet..."

CHAPTER SEVENTEEN

First Meet

Pure bliss. Those two words best described Beth's state of mind. Neither Beth nor Anne got any sleep because of their special "no pajamas" party. They knew they'd be paying the price for it, but agreed it was worth every penny. Fortunately, neither of them had tests or major assignments due, but they did have their first track meet.

"Are you nervous?" Anne asked Beth as they walked down to the track.

"I don't know…maybe a little bit. I know I've worked my ass off for weeks, so I think I'm physically ready, I just don't know if I'm mentally ready. I'm glad it's not a real meet. That helps calm my nerves."

"It is a real meet. It just isn't sanctioned. Our regular season may not start until November but take these meets seriously. Pretend each one is for division champs. That way when we get there, it will be old hat. Beth…you can do it, just give it everything you have."

"Anne…you do know we'll be competing on absolutely no sleep? You tired me out last night. I'll definitely be running on empty today," she said hardly able to contain her grin.

Anne lowered her voice, "I wish my roommates were gone, so I could tire you out again tonight."

The weather was perfect. Both track teams were spread out, stretching, running, jumping hurdles, throwing discus, and preparing for an array of other field events.

"I don't feel so good," Beth said as they ran slowly around the track to warm up.

"Oh no," Anne said laughing, "You're not serious, are you?" Beth laughed too but didn't answer the question.

Anne looked over and saw that Beth was white as a ghost. She grabbed her arm and led her off the track. "Let's visit the bathrooms."

They made it just in time. Beth spent the next fifteen minutes with either her head over the toilet, or sitting on the floor next to it, listening to Anne rebuild her confidence.

"I think I'm ready now... but don't tell anybody about this. Especially Carol."

Beth and Anne spent time watching some of the sprinters before they had to get ready for their own event. Occasionally at practice, the coach would have them train as sprinters to work on speed, but the mile was their specialty. When it was time for the mile run to begin, Beth still felt a little uneasy. But, when the gun went off, she forgot all about it.

Beth, Anne, and Carol pulled out in front immediately. Their pace was much faster than the other girls. All three ran side by side, but Anne and Beth would alternate the inside lane as they rounded the curves, so neither had a disadvantage. They started doing this technique at practice. At the half mile mark, all three had maintained their pace, and they had gained a significant lead on the other runners. As they rounded the curve for the final quarter mile, Beth moved into the inside lane. Unfortunately, she made her cut too close, and caught Anne's leg on Anne's back kick. Anne managed to get right back in stride, but Beth didn't. She fell hard onto the cinder track.

"Shit," Beth said as she quickly attempted to get back on her feet. But in her haste, she lost her balance and fell again. Anne stopped and ran back to help her.

"Go, don't wait for me!" Beth yelled angrily at Anne.

"Are you all right?" Anne said as she looked down at Beth's skinned knees.

"Yes! Damn it! Will you go!" Beth yelled as she got up and began running with a slight limp. Nevertheless, Anne didn't leave Beth's side. Even though they had had a strong lead, the other runners started passing them. Beth knew Carol was still the front runner and was going to take first place.

"Please Anne!" Beth begged as Anne jogged along next to her. You can't let everyone beat you!"

"Why not?" Anne said smiling at Beth.

"Because I don't want to hold you back!" she said as she stormed off the track, not bothering to finish the race. Beth headed straight for the bathrooms. Anne followed behind without saying a word.

"Is she all right?" Coach Ryan called out to Anne.

"Don't worry, she'll be okay. I'll take care of her," Anne assured.

Beth was sitting on the cold cement floor. She didn't look up as Anne walked over to her.

"Let me see your ankle. Does it hurt?"

"No…" she answered frustrated. "Oh Anne…how could I have done that? I'm so stupid. I'm not meant to compete in this sport." Anne knelt down next to Beth and took a look at her ankle.

"You'll live," Anne said smiling, "I think you hurt your ego more than your ankle. We do need to clean up your knees though. You've got blood running down your legs. I'm getting tired of seeing you covered with blood," Anne teased.

Beth said irritated, "Anne...I'm sorry I ruined it for you, but you could have kept running. I didn't need you to help me."

"If this weren't your first meet, I might have, but I could hear how hard you hit. It scared me. It sounded like when you hit your head on the log. I just didn't want to leave you."

Anne sat down next to Beth. "Look Beth, I don't even know what to say. It won't happen again. It was just a practice meet anyway."

"Oh yeah...right! Didn't you tell me to pretend every meet was for the division champs. I did a great job then huh?" Beth laughed at herself.

A big grin spread over Anne's face.

"What are you smiling about?" Beth asked.

"I just can't get over how cute you look sitting here on the floor. Why it wasn't that long ago you were sitting on the floor over there," she said pointing to a toilet.

Beth tried not to smile, but she couldn't do it. They both started to laugh.

"Okay," Beth conceded, "Maybe it's not the end of the world, but promise me Anne, that if I ever fall again, that you'll go on to finish."

"What if I'm the one who falls?" Anne asked, raising her voice but still smiling. Beth took a moment to think, "All right...let's do it this way...if by some strange chance we can't finish the race together, then the other will have to go on and win the race on their behalf."

"I'm in!" Anne agreed.

"Okay…let's make a promise. Give me your pinkie," Beth said as they hooked pinkies. Beth went first, "I, Beth Locke with an E," she paused until Anne stopped laughing. "promise to finish and try to win, any race that you can't, for whatever reason, no matter what." Anne watched Beth's face with a loving smile before she said, "And I, Anne Stetson, with an 'E' on Anne, promise to finish and try to win any race on your behalf, because I'm madly in love with you and would do anything for you." Then the two beautiful young women, sitting on the floor in only their skimpy track shorts and tops, smiled, leaned towards each other, and exchanged sweet, salty kisses, to seal their promises.

Anne stood up, reached out her hands, and pulled Beth up. "Come on, let's go get you cleaned up." Suddenly the bathroom door opened.

"Hey, I brought you some ice. Are you okay Beth? I'm really sorry about what happened, but don't worry we have plenty more meets. You'll have a lot more chances to prove how good you are." Beth smiled, but didn't trust the sincerity.

"Thanks Carol," Anne said. "You're absolutely right…"

CHAPTER EIGHTEEN

After a Fall

Thursday's practice was not going to be particularly demanding, but all the upperclassmen knew that the day after a meet, Coach Ryan would share her thoughts and expectations with selected individuals. It wasn't a fear provoking experience, but you knew she would share exactly how she felt about your performance and make clear her expectations. Coach Ryan had earned respect by the results of her instructions, and in the manner in which she expressed them.

During warm-ups, teammates were providing commentaries about particular performances, and sharing congratulatory remarks. Beth was standing off to the side with both knees covered with band-aids, and a wrap around her ankle. Anne was standing amongst the crowd and was her usual friendly self. No one seemed to question Anne about the incident on the track, but Beth was convinced they would interrogate her about her fall.

"Okay everyone, go to your assigned locations and let's get this practice started."

The team scattered and went to their designated areas to begin their drills.

"Anne, can I talk to you please?"

"Sure Coach."

"I'm sure you know what I need to talk to you about."

"Yes, I do. It concerns my performance at the meet yesterday," Anne said politely.

"Do you want to explain?"

"I made a bad judgement call. I went back when I should have gone forward."

"That's cleverly put. I know how protective you are of Beth, but it's time to let her fall and get back up on her own. She's tough. She's a fighter. Her past has taught her to go on, even when she's hurting more deeply than we can imagine. Someday, she will prove to everyone, that she can finish whatever it is she is determined to do."

"I agree. I'm sorry. I know she's a true champion Coach...I just need to get out of her way and let her prove it."

"You're a special person Anne, and she's blessed to have you as a friend," she said with sincerity. "Now...will you go get your little champion and tell her I need to talk to her?"

"Yes Coach? You wanted to talk to me?" Beth asked nervously.

"Yes...I have a few questions for you. First of all, how's your ankle?"

"Nothing serious, I can run full out on it by Monday."

"Okay...how are your knees?" Beth looked down at her "band-aid art", as she called it. "They're fine too."

"Okay...I'm glad to hear that. Now...why did you leave the track yesterday?"

"I'm really sorry. That's not like me. I'm not a quitter. I was just so embarrassed, and I felt like I let other people down," she said with obvious guilt.

"When you say 'people' you actually mean Anne, don't you?"

Beth didn't know how to respond. She panicked for a moment. Did she know she was in love with Anne? Beth mustered what courage she had to be as honest as she thought she could be. "I guess so. She's worked so hard with me. I felt horrible that I had disappointed her. I really did try to get her to keep running, but she wouldn't listen to me. I swear."

"I know Beth…but unless you're in too much physical pain, it's your responsibility to finish what you started. Sometimes you have to absorb the emotional pain and let it motivate you. I know you're not a quitter. You just remember that the next time you face a tough challenge."

"I will Coach. I promise, and I keep my promises." She meant it.

CHAPTER NINETEEN

Tennis Anyone?

Beth and Anne were looking forward to the weekend. They were caught up on schoolwork and didn't want to do anything they considered to be work.

Anne called Beth at nine o'clock Saturday morning, "I have an idea Beth," Anne said sounding excited. "Why don't we take a break from track and play some of the other sports we love. I miss playing tennis and I'm sure you're ready to get your hands on a lacrosse stick."

"I would love that! I have an extra lacrosse stick, and I'm sure you have plenty of rackets. Oh...I am so ready for this...let's do it!"

"All right...I'll come pick you up in a half hour and we'll head down to the lacrosse field first. Remember, bring me a lacrosse stick, and don't forget the ball."

Beth followed mockingly, "Okay, tennis this afternoon, and remember...bring me a racket and don't forget the balls." Anne smiled at Beth's teasing.

It was a beautiful sunny day. The field was wide open, and no one was around. Beth had grown to cherish their privacy. Beth was excited about teaching Anne how to play. It would be a welcome role reversal.

"Here...take this stick, it has a good pocket. It's my backup in case I need to get the other restrung."

"Thanks," Anne said as she took the stick, put the ball in it and started cradling it like an experienced player.

"Oh no...don't tell me you know how to play lacrosse too?" Beth said as she threw her head back in disbelief.

"I haven't picked up a stick in a very long time. I played when I was in middle school and up until tenth grade, before I gave it up for track. Believe me...I'm sure I'm very rusty."

"I somehow doubt that...is there any sport you don't play?"

"Of course there is ... I've never played any competitive softball. I know you did."

"Actually, I played mostly baseball when I was younger. I concentrated on lacrosse in high school. Nice try though."

Anne cradled the ball a few times and threw it at Beth, who caught it effortlessly and gracefully. Anne just laughed. "Come on... let's just throw for a while. I forgot how much I like this sport."

They spent the next hour and a half throwing, catching, scooping, and shooting at the goal cage. Their ingrained competitive nature surfaced as they challenged each other on just about everything. There was a lot of laughing though, and when the coast was clear...there was a lot of celebratory kisses.

"That was so much fun!" Anne said as they drove to get some lunch. Beth felt wonderful, and not just because she had so much fun playing, but because she made Anne happy. Seeing Anne smile, felt almost as good as a kiss.

"Let's eat, and then rest a bit before we play tennis. My roommates will be out of the apartment for a couple of hours this afternoon," she said as she grinned at Beth.

"We'll stop by the dorm so you can run in and get some fresh clothing, then come back to my place and shower."

"Hmmm…that could be a lot of fun. Will you wash my back?" Beth said, unable to contain her smile.

"Oh…I plan on doing more than that," Anne smiled mischievously. "Do you know what an 'afternoon delight' means?"

"No," Beth said naïvely.

"Well, you're going to find out…"

Neither of them had any rest, but they definitely felt energized and were ready to play tennis.

"Will you please be patient with me? I played tennis in gym class and with my brother a few times, but that's it."

"I don't care how you play. Let's just hit for a while. I can take a look at your strokes and help you." They hit the ball back and forth for a while. Beth was very quick at getting to the ball and could usually get it back over the net if she could reach it. Anne, however, never miss-hit a ball, and returned it with speed to the exact location she chose. Those locations were usually on the opposite side of where Beth was standing, or down the line, out of reach for any experienced player. They hit for a while, giving Anne the opportunity to give Beth some pointers on her grip, how to use spin, and ball placement.

As Anne met Beth at the net, she said proudly, "Once again, you've proven yourself to be one of the fastest learners I've ever known. You're already very good, and you just started. I'm serious…I know I tell you this all the time, but you really are one of a kind. That's just another reason I've fallen in love with you," Anne said smiling.

Anne worked on Beth's serve. It came naturally to her because it felt similar to the mechanics of throwing a ball. Her serve was powerful and becoming accurate quickly. They played a few games so Beth could get a refresher course on some of the rules and court courtesies.

"You ready for a break?" Anne asked as the sweat dripped down her face.

"Not really...but we can stop if you want," Beth said smiling. "This is fun. Now I'm determined to get better, so you better watch out. I'm coming after you..." Beth said pointing at Anne and smiling. Anne laughed at her and said, "Hey... I have an idea, but you may not like it," she paused and smiled at Beth.

"Oh no...this doesn't sound too inviting."

"Well...I think we would make a great doubles team. I would love to have you as my partner. Would you be willing to play a doubles match tomorrow?"

"Yeah...but who would we play against?"

"I know a really good player who I'm pretty sure would be able to pick up a decent playing partner."

"Who is she? Do I know her?"

"Well...when I played in high school, I was the number one seed. This girl was the number two and was determined to take my spot. We were very competitive with each other, her so more than me, if you can imagine that. She's a strong player and I know if I ask her, she will jump at the opportunity to play against me."

"Don't forget...you have me as a partner," Beth said jokingly.

"I wouldn't have asked you if I didn't think you were good enough."

"Well, okay but you still didn't tell me who she is. Do I know her?"

"Yes…it's Carol."

CHAPTER TWENTY

Let the Games Begin

"Hey Carol!" Anne called out when she saw Carol walking towards the courts.

"Hey guys…I hear you're up for a challenge," she said smiling.

"Beth and I are always up for a challenge! Right Beth?"

"Yup…that's me all right. I just love a challenge." Then Beth muttered quietly so Carol couldn't hear, "Especially when it's against you Carol."

"I want to introduce you to my friend Lex. We played tennis at my other college before I transferred here." Anne was the first to extend her hand and introduce herself. Beth followed suit.

"Let's warm up and you can let me know when you're ready to play," Anne said, "How about we start with best of three sets? Then, if we're not too exhausted we can play a one set round robin rotation." Everyone agreed including Beth, although she had no idea what they were talking about.

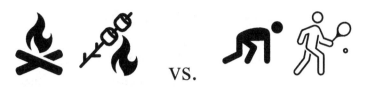

Anne and Beth vs. Carol and Lex

"Don't be nervous Beth. We're just playing for fun. Let your athletic abilities take over."

"Anne, I always do the best I can, but I've warned you, I'm a beginner. This was your idea."

"Okay…fair enough. I'm not worried though. You're my little phenom learner."

The two sides hit against each other for less than ten minutes when Beth confided in Anne, "Oh my gosh…they play like freaking professionals!"

"Well, they're really not that far out of that league. Don't worry though, Lex isn't as fast as you, so we'll hit to her as much as we can. Keep her running across the court. Keep it away from Carol at the net. She's tall enough to put most lobs away, and if you hit it short, she'll drive it right back at you and she'll do it with power."

"Oh boy…" was all Beth could say. They tossed the coin and Carol and Lex would serve first.

Carol served to Anne first, while Beth stood apprehensively at the net. Anne returned the ball back to Carol and kept her deep to prevent her from getting to the net. They rallied back and forth until Anne drove one past Lex and won the point. Beth kept her feet moving and followed the ball, but she didn't get a chance to touch it.

177

Now Carol would serve to Beth. The ball came in with a lot of speed and it seemed to skip off the court, but it was deep. The second serve was softer and hit to Beth's back hand. Beth loved hitting this shot because she got to use two hands, which made her feel like she had more power. She returned a hard shot to Lex and won the point. Beth was smiling now. She was beginning to love this game. It was easier than she thought. Beth and Anne won the first game.

Anne served the second game. They won easily because their opponents had trouble handling a serve that was both powerful and accurate. Not many balls were being hit to Beth, mostly because Anne placed them so they couldn't be. Beth's confidence was growing. Lex served the third game and Beth was starting to struggle returning balls. They lost that game.

"Your serve Beth. Remember…just do what comes natural to you. Pretend you're throwing a baseball, then get up to the net with me," Anne said encouragingly. Beth's serve was in and she charged the net. Carol hit the ball powerfully and directly back at Beth. Beth couldn't get her racket in place quick enough and the ball hit her hard in the stomach. You could hear the impact.

"Don't worry about it, Beth. She had a nice return," Anne said.

"Yeah…and I bet I get a nice bruise," Beth mumbled.

Beth did her best, but she couldn't seem to get the ball back over without hitting the net or hitting it directly to her opponents, who quickly put it away. Carol and Lex tried to hit every shot to Beth. Anne and Beth lost the second game.

Each game was close, and the aggressive spirit was growing stronger.

"You know I like to win Anne," Carol yelled across the net, "Especially against you two!" Then she gave Anne a big smile before she served to Beth and charged the net. Beth's return was too high, and Carol hit an aggressive overhead smash that landed right on top of Beth's head.

"Shit…" Beth called out, holding her head, and blushing with embarrassment.

"Are you okay?" Everyone yelled at the same time.

"Yes…let's just play. It's no big deal," Beth said perturbed.

"It's part of the game Beth, don't take it personally. She really didn't want to hurt you," Anne explained.

"Hmmm…no comment." Beth said making no eye contact with Anne.

The games and matches continued to be close. Beth took a beating from Carol. She was going to have more bruises than she could count, and that didn't include the bruising of her ego. Anne and Beth eventually won the match. As they shook hands at the net, Anne and Lex exchanged smiles, Carol and Beth did not. They barely made eye contact as Beth muttered, "nice match."

WINNERS: ANNE AND BETH

Anne and Carol vs. Beth and Lex

(Selected Conversations)

"You know we're going to get our asses kicked," Beth said smiling at Lex.

"That's probable, since Carol is almost as good as Anne, and Anne could have gone professional if she had dedicated herself to it. She beat a girl in high school that went on to be professional."

"How did you meet Anne?" Lex asked.
"We're on the track team together." Beth wasn't going to share anymore.
"How long have you been together?" Lex asked nonchalantly.
"Ahhh…" Beth was surprised and uncomfortable. "Why do you think we're together?"
"For one, Carol told me you were, and two, you act like you are." Beth just raised her eyebrows. Lex continued, "Don't worry, it's 'gaydar'. You will eventually develop it."
Beth opened up a little, "I feel really weird talking about this. Anne is my first. I'm kind of clueless. Besides, how do you count how long you've been together? First

crush, or first kiss, or the first time you tell each other you love them, or the first time you're intimate?"

Lex laughed, "I always use the first kiss, but everyone is different."

"Well… I guess I can tell you then, it hasn't been that long."

"I was with Carol for a short time, but she wasn't as serious about it as I was. She was honest though. At the time she told me she still had feelings for Anne."

"Believe me, she still does…" Beth said.

"Carol did ask me earlier today if I wanted to go out for dinner sometime. Maybe she's changing her mind…" Lex smiled.

"I hope so…" Beth said quietly.

"I think Carol called that ball out when it was clearly in," Beth said annoyed. "You know Carol better than I do. Do you think she would ever cheat to win?" Beth asked seriously.

"Carol is super competitive…but I doubt it. She likes to win though. She's an interesting person. One minute you think she would do anything to beat you, and the next you think she would do anything to protect and support you."

"I'm sorry we lost Beth, but I thoroughly enjoyed playing with you. You were a great partner. I can't believe you just started. You're amazing. I would love to play together again if you'll have me."

"I'd love it. You're a talented player. Thanks for your patience."

WINNERS: ANNE AND CAROL

Anne and Lex vs. Carol and Beth

(Selected Conversations)

"You ready to play little buddy?" Carol said as she gave Beth a slap on the back.

"As I told Anne, I always give my best, but remember I'm a beginner. I will make mistakes, but I won't be apologizing for every one of them. Are you okay with that?"

Carol smiled sincerely, "I like your attitude. I'll try to cover what you can't get to. You just keep the ball in, and I'll try to put them away."

"Do whatever you think you need to do to win. Unless of course it's cheating..." Beth grinned pretending she was kidding.

"Why don't you like me Beth? You know you're not hiding it very well."

Beth gave into the urge to be brutally honest. "Well...let's see. You patronize me at practice, I think you're capable of cheating to beat Anne and I, and oh yeah...I saw you kissing my girlfriend."

Carol looked at Beth for a moment, "I guess I can understand why you think that...but it's not fair. I don't patronize you. I think you have raw talent, and you haven't come close to reaching your potential. I don't cheat and I didn't know you were with Anne."

Beth didn't say anything. She picked up a ball and hit it back over to Anne so Anne could start serving.

Carol gave Beth a high five, "Nice shot Beth! We have a chance to catch up. Just keep doing what you're doing. We got this."

"Shit... I should have put that away!" Beth said angrily to herself.

"You're so cute when you get mad Beth..." Carol teased. "Let's see... I'm adorable, Anne's beautiful and you're cute. If we ever have a three way, we could call it an ABC."

Beth didn't laugh.

"Come on Beth...I'm just trying to get you to relax a little," Carol said smiling. Beth tried not to smile back, but she couldn't hold back a little grin. "That's very clever."

"You have to admit...that would be fun." Carol joked.

"In your dreams..." Beth said laughing. She couldn't believe she just said that out loud.

"Hey, you may already know this, but Coach Ryan told me we have to race against each other on Monday."

"I didn't know that."

"Yeah...just me and you. Anne doesn't have to run. I think it's because when you run with Anne, you two always beat me by about a second. I guess the coach wants to know if you can do it without Anne."

184

"Well...I guess we'll find out," Beth said confidently with a smile, but it was completely fake. She was scared to death.

"We have just tied them! We're even up! I think we can pull this off!

"I think we're running out of light and there're no lights on the court. How about we call it a tie, and finish it next weekend?" Carol called across the net.

"Good match Beth. We can finish them off next weekend. You did a great job. I can't believe you're a beginner. You were a great doubles partner. We would make a good team."

Beth knew she was being complimented but she could never imagine being a team with anyone but Anne.

WINNERS: TIE

CHAPTER TWENTY-ONE

Can Beth Beat Carol?

Monday came quickly and Beth was not looking forward to competing one on one with Carol. Without Anne by her side, she wasn't confident that she could beat her. She was concerned that, without Anne pacing and motivating her, she may not be able to post her best time.

When Beth told Anne about the race, Anne told her she wasn't aware of it, but she expected that it would happen sooner rather than later.

As Beth and Carol were completing their stretches, Coach Ryan approached,

"You two ready?" she asked.

"Yes," they said at the same time.

"Okay, take your spots on the track and we'll get you started." Beth's heart was pounding, but she knew Carol was nervous also.

"Anne will be clocking you, but she's not allowed to encourage you when you run past her," Coach Ryan said with a big smile. They both nodded they understood and took their places on the line. When the gun went off, Beth still wasn't sure what her strategy would be. She didn't know if she should take the lead or just stay even with Carol. She was caught off guard when Carol immediately pulled out in front and pushed their usual pace to the limits. Beth was determined to keep up with her. She stayed right behind her up until the half mile mark, and then pulled up next to her. That didn't last too long. Carol somehow managed to find enough drive, to take the lead by more than a couple of steps. Beth's lungs were fully taxed. She didn't know if she could keep this up for two more laps. She decided to keep on Carol's heels and then give it all she had in the final quarter, if she had anything left. She was already feeling like a failure. She was convinced Carol would beat her by more than a few seconds. Finally, as they headed into the final straight away, Beth gave it all she had. She pulled up even with Carol. She knew Carol was struggling too. She took a small lead and thought she might be able to keep it. They were less than ten feet from the finish line. Beth pulled back her arms and threw out her chest. She almost fell forward but managed to stay upright enough to slow down. After jogging a short distance, Beth

needed to stop. She leaned forward and planted her hands on her thighs, while she tried to catch her breath. She looked over at Carol. She was doing the same thing.

Beth took in deep breaths as she tried to get her body to recover. As her heart rate began to slow, Beth looked up and saw Anne just a few feet away.

"Did I beat her?" Beth asked quietly enough that Carol couldn't hear her.

"No…I'm sorry Beth, but it was close. She was less than a second in front of you."

"Crap. I'm never going to beat her."

"Don't worry Beth, it will happen. That's one thing I'm sure of. Just give it some time."

CHAPTER TWENTY-TWO

Photo Finish

Beth and Anne didn't talk much about Carol beating her the day before. Beth didn't want to. She was attempting to use it as motivation but was really struggling to make it real. The truth was, she felt embarrassed that she couldn't win without Anne.

The second meet was against a strong team. Their field event teams were weak, but not their sprinters and milers.

"We can do it you guys!" Anne said encouragingly to Beth and Carol as they set up by the starting line. They gave each other high fives and took their marks. Beth was next to Anne on one side and Carol was on the other. When the gun went off, the three of them took the lead and never looked back. Anne and Beth finished side by side and Carol almost even with them. Spectators could not determine who actually won the race, so they had to depend on the scoreboard that revealed that Anne and Beth had the exact finish times, with Carol a tenth of a second behind them. Beth was thrilled! She gave Anne a long hug, and Carol a high five. Beth was feeling great. Maybe she was meant to be a runner.

Thursday's meet was against State College, a school that was strong all around and had some of the state's top milers. Brittany Spence and Trish Marie were ranked as last year's number one milers. Everyone in the area that followed women's track and field knew their names. Similar to Anne and Beth, they usually finished side by side. Brittany had the most wins. They knew this could be the toughest challenge they would have during the preseason meets.

Anne, Beth, and Carol lined up as they usually did. Beth heard a hysterical fan yelling out to Brittany, "Take them down! Show them who's the real winner!" This only motivated Beth. She knew that Anne and Carol heard it as well, and that it would inspire them also.

When the gun went off, they scrambled for the lead position. The pace was fast, and State's runners were pushing harder than normal. It was most likely part of their strategy. The runners exchanged leads several times. There were some shoulder bumps amongst the pack, but nothing obvious enough to call for a disqualification. Beth had gotten bumped several times but was determined to ignore it. She was completely focused on giving it everything she had to give. She knew she had to keep it going for just ten more yards. She felt Brittany and Trish right next to her as they crossed the finish line. It was a big blur. She knew all five of them were about even, but she couldn't see clearly who won. It called for a photo finish. The photo revealed that Anne took first, Beth second, Brittany third, Carol fourth, and Tina fifth, all within less than one second of each other. It was the closest race they might ever have. All five of them posted the best times they had all season. Beth's body was so filled with adrenalin that she couldn't feel the pain of complete exhaustion.

"We did it Anne! I knew we could do it…and they thought they were going to 'put us in our place' didn't they?" Beth said referring to the comment made by one of State's fans.

"I never had a doubt…" Anne said smiling as she put her arm around Beth's shoulder. "When you put your heart and soul into something Beth, I don't think anyone is going to be able to beat you. You are my little champion…" Anne said grinning as she pulled Beth's head under her arm and ruffled her hair.

Friday's practice was held in the weight room. You could feel the excitement from the previous day's victory. A lot of attention was directed toward Anne and Beth for defeating their top rivals and breaking their own records. Carol had also beaten her best time, but it was not quite good enough to take a medal. She seemed disappointed and was quieter than normal. Anne went over to Carol and spoke to her privately for about ten minutes. Beth noticed Carol smiling a few times during the conversation. Beth decided it would be best not to ask Anne what she and Carol talked about.

Anne had to head home for the weekend, so they would have to postpone their tie breaking tennis match. Anne called Carol to let her know the situation and suggested she come up with another date for the match. Anne shared that Carol seemed disappointed but said she understood. She explained she would be seeing Lex this evening and would let her know.

Before Anne left, she and Beth found as much privacy as they could in Anne's BMW. Their goodbye kisses were exchanged behind the protection of steamed up windows.

CHAPTER TWENTY-THREE

Tennis Lessons with Lex

"Hey Beth, this is Lex."

"Hi Lex…it's good to hear from you."

"I have an idea…" Lex jumped right in.

"Okay…fill me in," Beth said very curious.

"Well…I thought I could give you some tennis lessons, and at the same time, I would have someone good to hit against. It could help both of us. We don't have to tell Anne. I think she would be impressed when she sees how good you have gotten." Beth didn't know what to say. She had to think for a moment.

"I guess that would be pretty cool if I suddenly could hit like a pro. She always tells me I'm the fastest learner she has ever known. This could totally impress her. Let's do it!"

"Okay, when can you get away?"

"Well…this weekend. Anne is going home."

"Okay, I can pick you up at your dorm and we'll go down to the tennis courts. I'll bring you a good racket. I'll need at least two hours to work on your groundstrokes. Does Saturday morning sound good? Let's say ten o'clock?"

"I'll be ready. Please don't tell Anne or Carol because Carol will rat us out. I really want to surprise Anne, and you better work me hard because otherwise she won't even notice a difference."

"Don't worry, I will."

Lex picked Beth up right on time and they headed to the courts. Beth was excited and highly motivated. She could picture the look on Anne's face when she saw how much she improved.

"You already have the basics, and you definitely have the speed and coordination. Now we have to get you to feel like that racket is an extension of your arm. If I can get you to put the right spin on the ball, you'll be able to hit it as hard as you want. The rest is touch. Kind of like when you're catching a lacrosse ball. It's all about touch. Something that you already feel and understand. That's why you'll get very good, very fast."

Lex hit balls, gave instructions, and rallied with Beth for nearly two and a half hours. The time went by so quickly that Beth didn't notice. Beth lived up to her reputation as a fast learner.

"Well...I think we better stop here so you can process what you've learned and give your body a break."

"Okay...I'm really enjoying this. I can actually feel and see my own improvement. You're doing a good job coach," Beth teased.

"Well...I've never had a better student and I've been teaching tennis every summer since I was in eleventh grade," Lex said with a big smile.

Beth's enthusiasm soared. "What are you doing tomorrow? Can we get together again? I loved hanging out with you. You're really good for me. I learned so much, so fast."

"That's fine with me. Are you sure you want to work with me again? I wasn't sure I was making a good impression or that you were actually enjoying yourself."

"No...I would really like to get together tomorrow, if it's okay with you," Beth said with a sweet smile. She was so excited that she almost couldn't wait.

"All right...it will have to be afternoon. I'll pick you up at three forty-five. That will give us some time before it gets dark."

Sunday afternoon's weather was grey and threatened to rain. Beth wanted to play. She was afraid Lex would cancel, but Lex showed up at three forty-five as planned.

They played until the sun was almost setting, and they would have played longer but the sky opened up and rain came pouring down. They ran for cover under a shelter next to the tennis courts.

"Oh my gosh! We barely made it!" Lex yelled because the sound of the rain on the tin roof was so loud.

"I'm drenched!" Beth laughed, looking down at her shirt that was so wet you could see her bra beneath it. "I didn't want to stop though. I was having so much fun! You're really something Lex and not just as a player but as a coach too."

"That's very nice of you to say. That's important to me. I really enjoy being with you."

"How long do you think we will have to wait before it eases up," Beth said as she turned and put her racket down on the bench. When she turned back around, Lex was standing close to her and looking into her eyes.

"Not long enough…" Lex said as she softly kissed Beth's lips. Beth didn't stop her. She didn't kiss her back, but she didn't push her away either.

"Oh my God…I can't do this. This isn't right. I'm sorry if I misled you. I'm in love with Anne," Beth said as she looked into Lex's eyes.

"Tell me you didn't enjoy that kiss…"

Beth couldn't say no. She didn't lie, "I can't do this Lex. I'm sorry. I really like you, but not in that way." Beth's heart was pounding.

"I understand...I'm sorry, I misread you. When you said it wasn't that long ago that you had your first kiss with Anne, I thought maybe you weren't committed yet." Lex looked into Beth's eyes and smiled as she teased, "It's just so hard not to want to kiss you. Carol was right...she told me it's hard not to be attracted to you."

CHAPTER TWENTY-FOUR

Best Friend and Lover

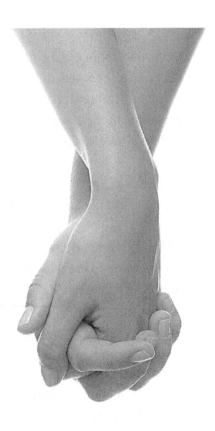

For the time being, Beth chose not to say anything to Anne about what had happened between her and Lex. She was considering if it would do more harm than good. She justified not telling Anne by the fact that she hadn't kissed Lex back. Then she remembered…Anne never kissed Carol back either. Beth knew she needed more time to figure out what to do.

Between track and maintaining good grades, Beth had little free time. What time she did have was almost always spent with Anne. She treasured those times. When the opportunities presented themselves, those moments were used for intimacy. Beth's love for Anne continued to grow deeper.

The days were becoming shorter and the evenings grew dark faster.

Anne called Beth, "Hey…do you want to walk downtown and get something to eat with me?"

"Oh, hi Anne," Beth laughed, "At least I think it's you."

"Well…who else would call asking you to dinner?" Anne teased back.

"Just the woman I love."

"Good, I'm going to come over in about twenty minutes and we can walk into town and grab some pizza."

Anne knocked on the door and Beth was ready to go. As they walked down a dimly lit street on the outskirts of town, Beth looked around first and then reached for Anne's hand and held it. She cherished the feeling it gave her, particularly when she could do it outside the confinement of one of their rooms.

"I love you Beth Locke with an 'E'," Anne said as she looked at Beth and gave her hand a little squeeze. "You know it still makes me quiver when you say you love me. I just can't believe that I'm with you. You're my best friend and lover," Beth said with a playful grin. Then she giggled, "That feels so weird saying, 'lover'."

"Why? I am your lover! It's not just physical either. I love you a hundred different ways...although the physical part is definitely one of my favorites."

Beth laughed then reflected, "I used to think that being with another woman was weird, but I never thought it was 'sinful.' I was always taught that God is all loving. He doesn't pick and choose who to single out as 'sinners' because they love someone. I don't understand why people think they're closer to God if they're straight. You'd think that people who have no problem cheating, or being abusive, would be called sinners. Not us! We're just two people in love. It's beautiful...we're not hurting anyone else. Why would anyone call us queer?"

"Did someone call us that?" Anne asked concerned.

"Well...you know what I mean..." Beth didn't want to lie."

Anne examined Beth's face closely looking for signs that Beth might be hiding something. "Beth, tell me the truth."

"Okay...I heard some girl in the locker room calling us queer. You're not going to believe this...but Carol told her to shut up. She stuck up for us...well at least for you."

"I do believe it. Carol has no problem sharing her thoughts."

"I just don't get it. It really pisses me off that people say stuff like that," Beth said angrily.

"You're right Beth," Anne said in a calming voice. "They don't understand so they have to put a label on it. It makes them feel more secure, I guess. Some people will see things differently after they get to know you and see you for who you are. Those who don't, aren't worth worrying about. Don't give them the power to fill you with hate."

"I hear you…I guess it's going to take me awhile to be as understanding as you. I still feel like kicking the shit out of them," Beth said with a devilish grin.

"Wow…you are one tough woman, aren't you?" Anne said laughing.

"When it comes to anyone hurting you, I am," Beth said grinning, then she took Anne's hand, brought it to her mouth and kissed it softly. "Just think of me as your bodyguard…" she smiled.

Anne hooked her arm in Beth's, and they walked without talking until they reached the lighted area. "By the way…I think that girl in the locker room who called us queer, was just jealous."

CHAPTER TWENTY-FIVE

Smokey the Bear

There were six track meets in the pre-season schedule that ended in late October. Beth and Anne finished in the top three positions in all of them except for the first meet, when Beth fell. Carol finished first in that meet but had taken fourth place in the meet against their toughest competitors from State College. Otherwise, Carol finished third in all other meets.

Beth and Anne continued to finish shoulder to shoulder, with Carol behind them by no more than half a second. It continued to be impossible to determine who the winner was without a photo finish. On two occasions, the first place finish was awarded to Anne, and the other two were recorded as ties. Their opponent's times were generally ten seconds or more behind them. Beth, Anne, and Carol were becoming recognized as top milers in the area, as were Brittany Spence and Trish Marie, from State College. Their only loss in pre-season was against Beth and Anne. They would face each other at least one more time during the upcoming winter indoor season, and hopefully in the championships. Beth and Anne were looking forward to the matchup.

Beth would soon need to decide if she was going to keep Forestry as her major. Her decision wasn't as difficult as she thought it was going to be. She loved some of her classes and was learning a lot more than she could have imagined. She found herself getting excited about making this a career. She knew that the jobs might not pay a lot, but at least she would get to be outdoors, in the woods, smelling the seasons and feeling she was doing something good for the world. Beth was tentative about telling Anne her decision, although there was no justifiable logic behind it. She knew Anne would be completely supportive and happy that Beth had come to her decision so easily. Beth however, worried that being a Forest Ranger would seem menial compared to Anne's profession as a doctor. She was afraid that a "Ranger" wouldn't be prestigious enough and might embarrass Anne when she introduced her to her colleagues. Beth was convinced she wouldn't fit in. She started thinking she might have to put, "The Lone" in front of "Ranger."

Beth told Anne she wanted to share something with her after practice. Anne seemed nervous until Beth explained that it was nothing to worry about, she just didn't want to share it in front of other people. After practice, Beth and Anne sat down next to the track.

"It's not a big deal Anne…I just wanted to tell you I've decided to stick with being a Forestry major."

"That's fantastic! I'm so proud of you!"

"I knew you would say that, but I have to tell you… I feel like it's very unimpressive compared to being a doctor. I don't want you to be disappointed."

"Beth…if you ever say that again, I'm going to kill you! I love the idea that you're going to be doing exactly what you love to do. That's always the most important thing. It doesn't matter if you're wearing a white lab coat or a Smokey the Bear hat, because what's important…" Anne started to say with a big grin on her face, but she never got to finish.

"Really!!! Did you just say what I thought you did?" she said as she grabbed Anne and wrestled her to the ground and sat on top of her. Anne was laughing so hard she couldn't say anything. Beth held Anne's wrists to the ground as she yelled and laughed at the same time, "I can't believe you made fun of a hat that I might actually have to wear!" They were both laughing so hard that tears started rolling down their faces. Beth rolled over to catch her breath. Anne did the same. They looked at each other with smiles so wide it almost hurt. Beth couldn't take her eyes off of Anne.

"I love you Anne, even though you're a jerk sometimes."

"I hope you honestly know how proud I am of you. This career is perfect for you, and anyone who hires you, will be glad they did. You'll do a great job," Anne said and then paused for a moment before she added, "I just can't wait to see you dressed up in your uniform. Oh my God…you're going to look so hot!" That comment earned Anne a punch in the arm.

"Honestly, Anne…I'm worried that my job might not be prestigious enough for you."

"Come on Beth…one job is no more important than another. Half of the doctors are stuck up insecure men anyway. I know you would love me just as much as I love you if I choose a different career. Wouldn't you?"

"Of course, but if you're looking for a rich girlfriend, I'm not going to be the one."

"Beth…by the time I get out of medical school, I will be so far in debt, that I can't even let myself think about it. Believe me…money is not what's going to bring us happiness."

Beth just smiled, "I love the idea that someday we'll live together in our own home in the woods, with a

couple of dogs, sitting around a fireplace, reminiscing about the time that we are living right now."

"It's going to happen someday Beth…I can just feel it."

Anne looked around to make sure no one was watching and gave Beth a soft kiss.

"I hope you're right…" Beth said as she stood up and reached for Anne's hands to help pull her up."

"I'm sure of it," she said as she gave Beth a warm smile. Then she added, "Now can you please tell me what size hat you wear so I can get you a Smokey the Bear hat that says, "Ranger Locke" on it?"

"No…you did not just say that!" Beth said loudly as she let go of Anne's hands and let her fall back down on her butt. Beth laughed loudly as she sat back down on Anne, held her wrists to the ground, and leaned forward so she could look directly into her eyes. Anne was giggling almost uncontrollably as Beth held her down. Her eyes were watering from laughter. Beth made herself stop laughing so she could say to Anne,

"Doctor Stetson…I want you to know that I'm going to love you forever," then sealed the promise with a kiss.

CHAPTER TWENTY-SIX

Tequila Hangover

There was a week break before the indoor track season was going to begin. Beth and Anne took advantage of the extra free time by doing some of the things they seldom got to do. One afternoon they went into town for an early dinner at a nice restaurant, and another was spent in the back row of the movies, so they could steal occasional kisses. Others were spent with friends who were also on break from their daily sports practices.

"We should have a party at your apartment Anne," Beth said as if it had just occurred to her.

"You mean this weekend because my roommates aren't going to be here, don't you?"

"It would be more fun without them. It's not that I don't like them, but they're different than most of our friends. I doubt they would like to do the same things we do," Beth said, adding enthusiastically, "Hey…we could make it an all girl's party."

"Who would we invite?"

"How about all the gay girls you know?"

"That's going to be an awfully small party," Anne laughed.

"Well…how many do you know besides Carol and Lex?"

"I knew more in high school than I do here. Abby and Mia are the only other ones that I can say for sure. There are a lot of girls who I suspect might be 'missing their calling' and will be coming out by the end of the school year, but I think it might only be the six of us at our party," Anne said smiling at Beth.

"You never told me Abby and Mia are gay. Are they together?"

"I don't think they were at our little party in the woods, but I found out they were together shortly after that. Who knows…maybe that campfire gave off some magical romantic smoke?"

"Can you call them and have them come over Saturday night? They can sleep over, so they don't have to worry about driving home."

"If you provide the entertainment, I'll see if I can get them to come over."

Beth had a big grin on her face, "I'm excited about this. This will be my first gay girl party. It's going to be fun!"

Beth and Anne made sure the apartment was ready for their little party. Anne always kept it clean and organized, so there was little cleaning to do. They made sure they had plenty of snacks and cold beer and waited for their company to arrive.

"I brought the Tequila!" Carol announced as she entered the apartment with Lex and held up the bottle. "You're going to love this stuff. It's sweet and goes down easy."

Lex proudly added, "I tried it last week and got a good buzz."

Abby and Mia showed up shortly after Carol and Lex, and the six of them sat around eating snacks and drinking beer. Beth asked about the Tequila, but Carol told everyone that the Tequila was going to be for "something special", but she wouldn't tell them what. Lex's grin made it apparent that she knew what Carol had planned.

Talk came easy. There was so much to share. They spent over an hour on the subjects of track, current gossip, and what their plans were for the Winter break. As the drinking increased, so did the volume of their voices and their energy. Beth was enjoying the company of other gay women. She loved the fact that she didn't have to hide her relationship with Anne. For the first time, she could hold Anne's hand in public. She had never felt so comfortable.

It wasn't long before Mia asked everyone how they had "come out" to each other, or the circumstances in which they had fallen in love. It turned out that Abby and Mia were each other's first love. They met on the track team and fell in love quickly. They said their first kiss was actually in the woods at the campfire party. Anne laughed as she reiterated that the campfire smoke must have been a magical love potion.

Lex explained that she had experimented with several girls in high school during her Junior and Senior years but had yet to fall madly in love. She smiled at Carol when she told everyone that she felt that "it was going to happen soon."

Anne revealed how she and Beth got together but left out some of the very intimate parts. She did, however, tell the story of the hunter and his young teenage boy at the pond. She had them laughing so hard they couldn't speak.

Beth was very curious about Carol's story. Anne had never shared much about it. Finally, it was Carol's turn. Carol started her story with an explanation of how in seventh grade, some of her friends would have a party at someone's house when the parents were away. They could usually only manage to steal a little wine or beer from their parent's liquor cabinets, but it was enough to convince them they were drunk. On special occasions, one girl would bring a bottle of Tequila. During those parties, they always played, "Spin the Tequila Bottle". She explained it didn't matter if it pointed to a boy or a girl, you still had to kiss that person. Boys didn't have to kiss other boys though. Carol said she loved when it pointed to another girl, even though she had to act like she didn't. She swore she tried to get just the right amount of spin so it would point to Taylor, the girl she had a crush on.

"You still didn't tell us who your first love was," Mia said after Carol finished telling them about Taylor.

"Well…it feels a little weird saying this…but since I'm a little drunk, I'll tell you. It was Anne. I fell madly in love with her when I was a Junior. She really was my first," she said as she looked over at Anne and smiled. Anne's face reddened as she smiled back. There was a moment of silence that was broken when Carol called out, "Okay… enough of this, let's play a game."

"Oh no…what do you have in mind?" Mia asked grinning. "I have a feeling it's going to get us in trouble."

"Well…you already know how to play because I explained it earlier."

"What?" Mia asked confused.

"The game 'Spin the Tequila Bottle'. I'll explain it more thoroughly so listen carefully. Every time the bottle points to you, you have to open the bottle and take a shot. I brought plastic shot glasses too." Beth and Anne just looked at each other. Everyone else was laughing.

"Come on…we're all drunk enough that we can enjoy it and it's not going to do any harm. No one is cheating, we're just having some fun."

"I'll do it," Lex said.

Abby and Mia looked at each other and Mia started laughing, "We're in. Neither of us have kissed another girl besides each other, so we might as well take advantage of the opportunity.

"How about you guys?" Carol said looking at Anne and Beth. Anne looked at Beth and shrugged her shoulders. "What do you think Beth? Are you feeling wild tonight?"

"I guess I don't want to be the only one sitting on the sidelines watching."

Carol jumped in, "Okay here are the rules. We'll use the rules we used in the seventh grade. If the bottle points to you, you take the shot before the kiss. You can only hold the kiss for five seconds and no French kissing unless you're fourteen or older."

"I think we need to change that one," Anne laughed.

"Oh, I almost forgot…everyone takes a shot before we start. I have two bottles of this special Tequila, so don't worry about running out."

Everyone sat on the floor in a circle. Each person got a small plastic shot cup and drank their shot.

"I just want to let everyone know…I'm a virgin Tequila drinker, but here goes," Beth said swallowing her shot. "This is good! It really is sweet."

"Okay let's play," Carol announced. "Beth you go first because you're the youngest." Beth spun the bottle and it pointed to Anne.

"Oh, that's not right…" Lex kidded.

"Oh, I just won the jackpot," Anne bragged as she opened the bottle and poured herself a shot and drank it quickly. Beth moved over to Anne and whispered, "I love you," before she gave her a soft kiss.

"That's almost like cheating…they get to kiss every day," Lex joked.

Carol jumped in, "Okay…we didn't have that problem in seventh grade because none of us were together, so we'll change the rules. If you get your partner, you have to take a shot and spin again."

"Oh my God…we're going to get so drunk we won't know who we're kissing," Abby said laughing.

"Okay, your turn Anne because Beth spun you." Anne spun the bottle and it landed on Abby. Anne moved over and kissed Abby softly on the lips. Beth watched closely and wasn't sure what she was feeling. It was sexy seeing Anne kissing another girl, but there was a touch of discomfort that went with it. It wasn't long before Lex's bottle pointed to Beth.

"Oh no…this is going to be good," Carol kidded. It seemed she already knew Lex had a crush on Beth.

Lex came over to Beth as Beth downed her shot. Lex gave her a deep kiss that lasted the full five seconds.

"That's cheating!" Carol yelled laughing. "I saw you two French kissing."

Beth smiled and started laughing as she prepared to spin. The game continued and so did the drinking.

Beth's bottle eventually ended up pointing to Carol. Beth hadn't been looking forward to this, but she knew it was coming. Beth went over to Carol and placed her lips on her mouth. Carol's lips felt soft and warm, and Beth held the kiss a little longer than she had intended. Beth hadn't expected to feel anything, but she did. They both just laughed it off when they were done.

"Finally!" Lex called out when she spun Carol. "Hey, can we change this game to "seven minutes in heaven?" Lex teased.

"You and I have already done that one Lex…and we didn't need a bottle," Carol kidded. Everyone laughed hard. That kiss lasted well over the five second mark.

It must have been Carol's special touch that stopped her bottle, so that it was pointing directly at Anne. This was the first time Carol and Anne were going to have to kiss. Carol moved slowly over to Anne and looked lovingly into her eyes before she gave her a long soft kiss. Anne blushed and Carol smiled as their lips finally separated. Beth could feel how much Carol enjoyed that moment. Beth did not.

The game continued into the night, and so did the drinking. Anne was the first to announce that she thought the game had gone on long enough and everyone most likely had too much to drink already.

"I just want to let everyone know that I am officially drunk," Beth announced. She was louder than normal, but she didn't sound drunk. She didn't slur her words, and as a matter of fact, she made herself quite clear. "This is also my first official 'gay girl' party and I had no idea how much fun they could be. This beats any other party I've ever been to. I didn't realize all the fun I had been missing out on all these years." Abby and Mia laughed and nodded in agreement.

Beth continued, "We're going to have to do this again. Carol and Lex, can you make sure you bring this same stuff?" she said as she held up the bottle looking for the name on it.

"I think I'm in love with this Tequila."

"Go easy Beth...remember you're a virgin---," Anne's next word was going to be "drinker", but Beth cut her off.

"You don't have to tell everyone I'm a virgin. I went out with Marco that night to have sex, but I couldn't do it." Beth said laughing.

"Beth!" Anne yelled surprised but with a grin on her face.

"Oh...do tell more," Lex urged her on.

"That's enough Beth, you don't need to share everything."

"Well, it's true...I bet everyone here has had sex but me." No one disagreed with her.

"Tenth grade for me," Carol said.

"Eleventh for me," Lex said.

"Senior year for both of us," Abby and Mia said. Anne didn't say anything.

"Anne...you never told me when you first had sex," Beth said eyebrows raised.

"Come on Anne...when did you first do the dirty?" Lex said smiling.

Anne hesitated and seemed like she really didn't want to share, but finally submitted to the pressure.

"I was only in 8th grade. I didn't like it and it was his idea, not mine. He was five years older than me. He swore he thought I was much older. Believe me...Beth it's not worth it unless you love someone..." Anne said with all seriousness. It was not intended, but that moment put a damper on the party.

Everyone helped clean up and told each other what a good time they had before they headed into their bedrooms. Anne led Beth into her bedroom. Beth was drunk, but not sloppy drunk. She was still sweet and couldn't get the smile off her face as she repeatedly told Anne how much she loved her. Beth took off her shirt and plopped down on the bed. Anne tried to talk her into changing but was unsuccessful.

Beth woke late Sunday morning.

"Oh, my head hurts..." she moaned.

"Well it should," Anne said smiling at Beth who was still lying face down on the bed.

"Well...did I at least have a good time?" Beth said as she tried to laugh.

"I believe you did...but you're going to be paying for it today. You officially have your first 'Tequila Hangover'."

CHAPTER TWENTY-SEVEN

In Your Arms

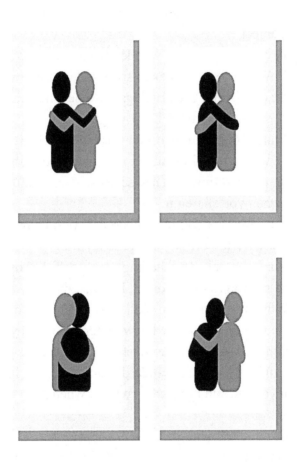

By late afternoon on Sunday, Beth felt like her old self again and didn't want to waste the afternoon. The temperature outside was crisp, but the sunny skies kept it warm enough to be inviting. Beth suggested to Anne that they go for a walk around the campus to take advantage of the beautiful weather. Beth had an ulterior motive too. She wanted a safe and comfortable environment to bring up a sensitive subject.

They took a seat on a wooden bench in the campus courtyard. After a few minutes of small talk about how picturesque everything was, Beth gave Anne's hand a gentle squeeze and looked at her lovingly.

"Anne, I don't know if you want to talk about this…but I've been thinking about what you said at the party about the first time you had sex. I saw how emotional you were when you shared it."

"I'm surprised you remembered. I would have thought you were too drunk." Anne said jokingly.

"No, I remember all the important stuff. I know that it was hard for you to talk about it. I feel badly."

"Why? It was my own fault. I went out with him."

"He was older, and he knew better. He raped you Anne," Beth said softly but seriously.

"I guess by today's standards that's true, but I don't know if anyone would have believed that when it happened."

"Did you tell your parents?"

"Oh God no. They would have killed me. They didn't even want me dating until the ninth grade." Beth didn't say anything. She let Anne continue.

"They think of me as the all-American girl and I never want to disappoint them. Knowing I had sex at all, would've killed them. Knowing it was with a nineteen-year-old...oh my God I can't imagine how they would have reacted," Anne said shaking her head. "Let me take that back. I know what my father would've done. He would have been knocking on that guy's door with a loaded shotgun in his hand."

"Can't we do something about it?" Beth said looking into Anne's eyes with genuine concern.

"I doubt it. I don't want to anyway. I don't even like to think about it. I just want to forget it. I felt horrible about myself. I felt like I was some kind of slut."

"Don't say that Anne! It wasn't your fault. You were just a child!" Beth said firmly. She noticed that Anne was trying to hold back tears. Beth reached over and held Anne tightly in her arms. Anne put her head on Beth's shoulder and began to cry. Beth never saw Anne cry before. She had never seen her so wounded and vulnerable. She didn't know how to comfort her.

"Anne...I will do anything to help you," Beth said quietly keeping her arms wrapped around Anne.

"There's nothing I want you to do. I just want to forget it," Anne said sadly.

"Will you let me know if you ever want to talk about it?" Beth whispered.

Anne didn't respond for a moment until she stopped crying. She sat back and wiped away the tears that were still rolling down her cheeks.

"I will Beth...but not now, I'm so happy being with you that I just don't want to think about it. Maybe sometime later…but for right now, I just want to enjoy you," Anne said as she kissed Beth on the cheek.

"I want you to know Anne…that no matter what, I'll be here for you."

A soft smile came across Anne's face, "I'll always be here for you too Beth."

Beth placed her hand on top of Anne's. "I know you will. We will always have each other…always."

Anne used her sleeve to wipe away any leftover tears then quietly said, "Thank you for taking care of me Beth. It's hard for me to talk about it. I'm a little embarrassed that I cried, but if I had to…I'm glad it was in your arms."

CHAPTER TWENTY-EIGHT

A Piece of the Puzzle

In November, because of the colder weather, track was moved to the indoor facility. The energy and excitement of the first day back to practice was evident. Groups of athletes tended to corral according to their event. Abby and Mia, who were relay sprinters, joined Beth and Anne. As soon as Anne saw Carol enter the complex, she waved her over.

"Did everyone have an exciting weekend?" Carol said with a mischievous grin. Abby and Mia chuckled and nodded yes. Anne and Beth just smiled.

"Well, I'm glad everyone enjoyed themselves. We just might have to do it again," Carol beamed.

"I didn't enjoy myself too much the next day," Beth laughed. "Anne told me I had a Tequila hangover. Is that somehow different than all the other hangovers?"

"It must be," Mia said, "because Abby and I had it too and it was much worse than any beer hangover I've ever had. How about you Carol, how'd you feel the next day?"

"Actually, I felt pretty good. Either my body has gotten used to it, or I didn't get to drink enough because that damn bottle wouldn't point my way."

"I think you got your fair share of kisses," Abby kidded.

"Never enough…never enough," Carol grinned.

The "Spin the Tequila Bottle" adventure wouldn't be shared with anyone else. It was a communal secret.

There would be a week and a half of practice before their first indoor meet. It would be an invitational meet and runners from a variety of colleges would be competing.

Beth and Anne stayed late every day for additional training and ran on weekends. Carol joined them on their weekend runs. Beth tolerated it because she knew Anne believed it would benefit them all.

The day before the meet, Beth admitted to Anne that she was almost as nervous now, as she was at her very first meet. Anne recapped that the track was still the same size, and she would be competing against the same runners, so the results would be at least as good. She reminded Beth that she would be right by her shoulder, like a guardian angel protecting her from falling again. She said encouragingly, "We're going undefeated this season Beth, so you better be ready. You need to believe in yourself."

The first meet was close, but Anne, Beth, and Carol took the top three spots. Anne was first, Beth second, and Carol a close third. There were more sports reporters than usual because it was an invitational. Anne and Beth were asked to do a brief interview concerning their successful track records and their shoulder to shoulder finishes. Anne did most of the talking. She credited Coach Ryan, praised her teammates, even mentioned Carol by name. When asked about their dual finishes, Beth spoke up, "We give it everything we have, every race. Anne motivates me. She brings out the best in me and if I don't keep up, she'll kill me," Beth said grinning at Anne.

The second meet was also an invitational meet and Carol's previous college would be participating. It would be the first time they would be competing against them. Carol never fully shared with anyone why she transferred except to say, "It was a better fit."

Carol had been watching the sports complex doors as members of the other team started entering. Anne noticed and walked over to her, "You seem nervous. Are you ready for this?" Anne said smiling as she put her arm around Carol's shoulder.

"I'd be lying if I said I wasn't a little nervous. Most of them aren't mad at me for transferring, but the coach wasn't happy about it."

"Well…you needed to do what was best for you. Do you have any regrets about coming here?"

"No, not at all. I miss my friends but I'm happier here."

"That's all that matters. Your friends will understand, and your coach will have to deal with it," Anne said giving Carol's shoulder a squeeze. "You're going to do great today Carol. Just run your race and I'm sure you'll have no problem crossing that finish line in front of all of them."

"Including you I hope," Carol said grinning.

"You never know…but I'll do my best to make sure you don't," Anne teased.

Carol received a lot of long hugs and warm welcomes from her former teammates. It seemed Carol was well liked and respected. Her previous coach didn't hug her, but he did extend his hand, when he greeted her. They spoke for a few minutes before Carol had to get ready for her race. They shook again and Carol gave him a sincere smile before she jogged away. Everything seemed to be okay.

As the runners began to take their positions on the line, Anne, Beth, and Carol gave each other high fives as part of their pre-run ritual. Beth was nervous as usual, but she was surprisingly more nervous for Carol. She wanted Carol to beat her former teammates. She wanted them to know that Carol had transferred to a better school, but she still wanted to know why Carol chose to transfer. She had always assumed it was her desire to be near Anne, but as she grew to know Carol a little better, she wasn't convinced it was the only motivation. Beth realized that Carol was more complex than she had originally thought.

When the gun went off, the three of them immediately took the top positions, but this time it was Carol who took the lead. Carol's pace was faster than they had ever run before. Beth was worried that it was in poor judgement and chose to continue at the pace that she and Anne had always run. Carol continued to push herself. Beth knew that Carol was taking a chance because she might fade in the end. As they entered the last quarter mile, Carol still held a strong lead, but Beth sensed that she would be slowing soon. She was right. She and Anne were right behind her, followed very closely by two of her former teammates. As they came down the stretch, Beth and Anne were almost even with Carol, and so were two opponents. As they crossed the finish line, Beth had no idea who won. As usual, it was too close to call. The photo finish seemed to take forever. The final results…Anne in first place, Beth and Carol tied for second. Carol had beaten her best time and Beth had tied her best time. Beth wasn't at all disappointed with the results. She wasn't upset that she hadn't beaten Carol. The excitement on Carol's face was worth it.

After their race, the three of them went over to watch the sprinters. An attractive young woman from the other team came over. Carol introduced her to them as her former teammate, Nicole. Carol and Nicole excused themselves and walked over to the side of the bleachers. Beth knew she shouldn't do it, but she watched them closely. Their interactions seemed uncomfortable. Carol was not smiling, and the other woman seemed upset. She saw Carol reach for Nicole and hold her. Nicole seemed to be crying. Beth tried to get Anne's attention so she could help interpret what she was witnessing.

"That's really none of our business Beth…but if I were to guess, I think Carol may have broken her heart."

After the meet, Carol invited Anne and Beth back to her dorm room so she could talk with them. Beth was both curious and concerned. She had never seen Carol this serious before. Anne said she wasn't sure what Carol wanted to talk about, but she could tell Carol was upset about something.

Since Beth lived in the same dorm, she and Anne showered quickly and went to see Carol. Anne had been to Carol's room before, but this was the first time Beth had seen it and she was genuinely impressed. It didn't look like a typical dorm room. It looked like it came straight out of a magazine. Beth could only imagine what Carol's family home must look like.

"Can I get you guys anything?" Carol asked. Beth and Anne agreed that they were fine. Carol seemed nervous.

"What's wrong Carol…I know something's bothering you," Anne asked sweetly.

"Well…you know when I told you I was nervous about the meet? It wasn't just because of seeing the coach again, or that I was afraid I was going to lose. I was nervous about seeing the girl I introduced you to…Nicole." Beth and Anne didn't say anything. They let Carol continue.

"Nicole and I were together for a while. I met her through track. She's really a good person. She's sweet, smart, and super athletic. I can't say anything bad about her. She treated me well. I thought I was falling in love with her, and I told her so. She told me she'd been in love with me from the first time we met, and that I was her first true love. Things were fine in the beginning, but I started to feel like I was missing something. I kept trying to convince myself I was in love…but I just wasn't feeling it. I wanted to somehow make myself feel the love, but I knew it wasn't going to work." Carol paused for a moment and looked at Anne, "Am I making any sense? Am I just a terrible person? I didn't want to hurt her. I really tried, I swear, but I knew I couldn't continue like that. I had to tell her.

"Carol…don't beat yourself up. You can't help how you feel. At least you were honest," Anne said supportively.

"Unfortunately, she didn't handle it well," Carol said sadly, "I told her how beautiful and wonderful she

231

was, and I truly meant it. I said that remaining friends was extremely important to me and I meant that too. She's such a good person. You know that line, 'it's not you, it's me,' that people say when they're breaking up? Well, it's true."

"Carol, you didn't do anything wrong. I'm sure she'll eventually get over it," Anne said softly as she placed her hand on Carol's knee.

Carol shook her head, "I don't know, I don't think I handled it right. I think I did everything wrong." Carol was fighting off tears.

"She called me a lot, she wrote me notes, and she would just show up at my room. She kept saying she didn't understand why I didn't love her, and how much I hurt her." Carol couldn't hold back her tears. "She said this was killing her…she said she couldn't take it—" Carol couldn't get out anymore words. Anne went over and put her arm around her shoulder. "Anne," Carol said crying, "she tried to kill herself and it was my fault!"

"No, no, Carol don't say that. It wasn't your fault. You didn't do anything wrong. You can't control what other people do," Anne said soothingly as she pulled Carol tight against her. Carol cried harder, and it took a moment for her to be able to talk again.

"I found her lying on the floor in her room! It was my fault…I hate myself for it." Anne continued to try to calm her.

"She called me to say goodbye and tell me she loved me. I ran to her room hoping that she really wasn't going to hurt herself, but when I got in the room, I found her lying on the floor. I didn't know if she was alive—" Carol was sobbing so hard she had to stop talking.

232

"Carol, I know it hurts, but you have to know it wasn't your fault," Anne said as she held Carol.

"It was horrible...she was just lying there. I shook her and yelled at her, but she didn't move...I couldn't get her to say anything."

"It's okay...it's okay," Anne whispered as she comforted her.

"I called 911 and held her in my lap until they got there. It seemed like an eternity." Carol didn't say anything for a moment as if she were reliving the nightmare.

Beth tried to comfort Carol, "You did the right thing Carol...everything you did was exactly what you should have done."

"I didn't want to hurt her...and I almost killed her."

"No, you didn't. You saved her life," Beth said.

Carol was speechless as she attempted to stop crying. Anne held her tight. Carol's tears slowed and she tried to regain her composure.

"They pumped her stomach and said there was no serious damage, but if it had been another half hour, it would have been a different story." Carol looked directly at Anne, "I'm trying to convince myself that it wasn't my fault, but my heart aches so much that I just can't believe it."

"It'll take time Carol...but it will happen," Anne said quietly.

"I went to the hospital to see Nicole, but I didn't go in because I thought it would hurt her more. I just didn't know what the hell I was supposed to do. Her parents were a wreck. They were in complete shock. It was killing me watching their pain. They didn't know anything about us.

What was I supposed to tell them? I let them think she was just depressed, so she tried to kill herself."

"Carol…you didn't do a single thing wrong. You really didn't. You have to believe that!" Beth emphasized.

"I didn't know what to do. Should I stay and be there for her? Or should I get out of her life? You know…just leave and go to a different college. I didn't know what to do and I had no one to talk to about it. I kept thinking, am I helping her by leaving or am I just a coward who doesn't want to deal with it?"

"Well, she's back at school and running track again, so it seems this nightmare might be coming to an end," Anne said.

"She does seem a little better. She told me she got help. She's seeing a therapist and they have her taking antidepressants. She even apologized to me at the track when we spoke."

"Good…good. Things are going to be okay. I know they will Carol. Just give it some more time," Anne said smiling.

"I'm afraid to get involved with anyone again," Carol admitted.

"Don't say that. It might take a little more time…but you will. I'm sure. You're just too hot a catch to stay single," Beth teased trying to make Carol laugh. She didn't get a laugh, but she did get a little smile.

"You're the only people who know anything about this. I've been keeping this to myself and it's been killing me. I knew I'd see her at the meet today. I was afraid I was going to lose it when I saw her, but after talking to Nicole, I started feeling a little better. Not much, but at least it's a start. Nicole told me that maybe someday we can be friends again."

"It'll work out, don't worry," Anne said tenderly.

"Thank you. Thank you both. I've embarrassed myself…but I just needed someone to talk to. You two were the only ones I felt comfortable enough to tell. I hoped you'd understand. Now you know why I transferred here. I'm sure you were a bit puzzled, but at least now you have the missing piece." Then Carol's eyes welled up again, "Thanks for listening to me. I love you guys."

CHAPTER TWENTY-NINE

Family Visit

After practice on Tuesday, Anne told Beth she was going to invite her parents to come see the track meet that was scheduled for Saturday. This was the largest invitational meet before the Christmas break. She practically begged Beth to call her brother and see if he and his wife could come and watch Beth compete. Beth was concerned about the inconvenience of the seven hour road trip they would have to make. She wasn't convinced they would even enjoy it. Her brother always said he liked to see her compete in sports, but she figured he was just being kind.

Beth was apprehensive when she made the phone call home. She was pleasantly surprised that her brother seemed genuinely excited and appreciative of the invitation.

She called Anne as soon as she got off the phone with her brother, and they eagerly began making plans for the entire day.

As Saturday approached, Beth found herself getting nervous about her brother's visit, more than about the meet itself. She loved her brother and his wife dearly and thought the world of them. She never wanted to disappoint them, and as of yet, never felt she had. She was concerned that he might suspect something about her relationship with Anne, and that it would upset him.

The plan for Saturday was for all of them to meet at the field house about an hour before the meet. This way they could be properly introduced and have a chance to get acquainted with each other. After the meet, Beth and Anne were going to give them a quick tour of the campus, including Beth's dorm room, and then head back to Anne's apartment so Beth and Anne could shower and get ready to go out to eat.

"I'm really nervous," Beth admitted as they drove to the field house, "I hope you like my brother."

"If he's anything like you, I'm sure I'll love him."

"I hope your parents like him too. He's just an easy going type of guy, very unpretentious. He gets along with everyone. He's a construction supervisor. Do you think that's good enough for your parents?"

"That's not fair Beth. You know my parents. They don't care about what job you have. They just care that you're a decent, honest and hardworking person."

"Well, it's too late anyway. They'll be at the track in an hour."

"There's your Mom and Dad," Beth pointed out as she saw them enter the track complex. Anne ran up to greet them and brought them over to where Beth was standing. At about the same time, Beth saw her brother and his wife come through the door.

"Hi Mr. and Mrs. Stetson," Beth quickly put out her hand and shook hands with both of them. "You'll have to excuse me I see my brother over there."

"Hey David," Beth smiled and gave him a big hug."

"Oh my gosh…I can't believe it! My baby sister looks so grown up," David said as he held Beth close and gave her a kiss on the top of her head. "We miss you. Our home seems empty without you."

"I miss you guys too," Beth said as she turned and hugged her sister-in-law Judy. "Come on, let me introduce you to my best friend and her parents."

Introductions were made and the families seemed to be comfortable immediately. Before Beth and Anne left for the locker room, Beth heard Anne's father and her brother agree that it was so nice to see "their girls" so happy.

The field house was already crowded with spectators, athletes, and reporters from the local papers. The two families found seats in the front row bleachers. The meet was scheduled to start at three o'clock. To an inexperienced spectator, it looked like disorganized chaos. It seemed impossible that everything would somehow be perfectly coordinated in thirty minutes. Spectators walked about aimlessly as runners stretched out on the floor anywhere there was enough space to fit them. Some runners were sprinting, some jogging slowly, some in one direction and others in the opposite. Field event athletes were either throwing or jumping. Some jumping hurdles, others using poles to clear their entire body over a bar more than fourteen feet in the air.

Beth and Anne, now dressed in their skimpy running outfits, waved to their families as they ran past during their warm-ups.

"I think they're going to get along," Anne said to Beth as they jogged together.

"I'm nervous about everything right now," Beth admitted.

"Beth…you just need to get focused on the meet."

"Okay…I'm trying. What if we don't win? I'll be so embarrassed and feel like I disappointed them," Beth said anxiously.

"We're going to do fine. Remember…we're a team. We'll do it together, like we always do."

Amazingly at three o'clock, everything fell into place. The field events were starting, and the track was cleared and ready for the races. The mile run would be the fifth event.

Beth and Anne took their positions on the track. Their lanes were side by side and Carol was a few lanes over. When the gun went off, Beth, Anne, and Carol quickly became the front runners. The competition was strong, but Beth and Anne had beaten all of them in the preseason. There was one exception, a new girl they had never seen before. For the first three laps their positions had not changed. Beth, Anne, and Carol had extended their lead, but the new girl was right behind them. As they turned into the final lap, the new girl pulled out to pass them and bumped Beth hard with her elbow. Beth was knocked off to the side and lost about one step. This was a significant disadvantage when fractions of seconds were the determining factor in who was considered a winner, and who was a loser. Beth was infuriated but refused to let this stop her from finishing next to Anne. She could picture their families sitting in the bleachers watching and cheering as she and Anne finished shoulder to shoulder in first place. Somehow that image helped her find strength she never knew she had. She was completely depleted when she crossed the line, but she knew she had Anne's shoulder by her side. Her legs were about to give out, but she managed to stay upright long enough for Anne and Carol to reach her and help hold her up.

"Did we do it?" Beth asked as they helped her walk.

"We all beat her," Anne smiled.

Carol jumped in, "I saw that girl elbow you. I don't know how you managed to recover but you did it Beth." Carol needed a couple of deep breaths before she added, "You should be very proud of yourself."

"You made your brother and his wife proud too," Anne smiled.

"We make a good team, don't we?" Beth grinned.

After a couple of minutes Anne told Carol she could take care of Beth from here on. Carol helped place Beth's arm around Anne's shoulder and Anne wrap her arm around Beth's waist. They just walked for a while without talking until Beth seemed recovered.

"I feel better now…I can walk on my own."

"I know. I just don't want to let go. I kind of like walking in front of hundreds of people with an excuse to put my arm around you," Anne said smiling.

Beth laughed but still wanted to relive the victory, "We did it, didn't we…" Beth beamed, "We really are a team. If you hadn't reminded me of that before the meet, I wouldn't have been able to catch up to you. I would've felt too guilty. Guilt is a great motivator, isn't it?" Beth teased.

As soon as Beth and Anne left the track, they were greeted by excited family members.

"What a race! Oh my gosh Beth, I knew you were fast, but I didn't know you were that fast! I'm so impressed!" David gushed.

"I didn't expect it to be that exciting to watch!" Judy added.

Mr. Stetson put his hand on Beth's shoulder and said, "I saw that young lady bump you. She could've knocked you over. I can see you're no quitter."

David, still excited, asked, "Do you always finish like that? Side by side? I don't even know who got first place."

"We don't usually know until we see the results on the board," Anne said.

"They posted your scores already. Believe it or not...you two and Carol were all tied." Mrs. Stetson informed them.

"You two make great partners," David said enthusiastically.

"I don't think I could be as successful as I am without Anne running right by my side. I'm scared she'll kill me if I don't keep up."

"I'm not that bad," Anne said as she gave Beth a gentle punch in the arm.

"Ouch...you see how she motivates me," Beth said unable to hold back a big grin.

Anne invited everyone to join them while they cheered on their teammates in other events. This was the first track meet that David and Judy had ever attended. They seemed sincerely interested and excited. Judy was full of questions that Beth was more than happy to answer. She loved being able to share at least one important part of her life.

After the meet, they visited Beth's dorm and got a short tour of the campus. Then they headed over to Anne's apartment to get ready to go out to eat. They had made reservations at a nice restaurant in town. It was a beautiful cool evening, so Anne suggested they walk. The trip was full of conversations between everyone. Beth was glowing from the excitement of the win and the feeling of love coming from her family. Anne joked and laughed with Beth most of the way, especially after listening to funny childhood stories from Beth's brother. He told her one about the time they were out to dinner at a restaurant they had never been to before. Beth, who was about fifteen at the time, excused herself to go to the bathroom. When she returned, she asked why there were urinals in the bathroom. He said he didn't have the heart to tell her she had mistakenly gone into the Men's room.

Everyone exclaimed how much they enjoyed their dinner and agreed it had been an absolutely wonderful day. The atmosphere was filled with delight. Mrs. Stetson was the first one to insist that they should all get together again soon. The rest of them simultaneously agreed, "Yes, let's do it again!"

As they walked back, David pulled Beth to the back of the pack and put his arm around her shoulder.

"I could never be more proud of you Beth. You are so special to me that I don't know how to explain it. I can only hope you can feel how much I love you. I'm thrilled that you're happy and pleased that you have found such a special friendship with Anne." David stopped walking and took his arm off Beth's shoulder. He reached for her hands as he looked lovingly into her eyes. He spoke softly, "I can tell she makes you happy. I can feel the caring and love between you. Never be ashamed of that and remember you can never disappoint me. Just be who you are. That's perfect enough."

Beth couldn't speak for a moment because she was fighting back tears.

"Thank you, David…thanks for loving and supporting me. That means more to me than you can possibly imagine," Beth said as her eyes became watery.

David just smiled and put his arm back around her shoulder and gave it a squeeze. He kept his arm like that the rest of the way back to the apartment.

The Stetson's were driving home that evening, and after some discussion, the Locke's decided they would return home as well. They had considered staying at a hotel for the night but decided to drive through and sleep in late when they got home.

Beth felt the sadness of their departure. David and Judy's visit reminded her of how much she cared for them. They had helped her through her depression after her parent's death and they filled that void with many happy memories. The goodbye hugs and kisses that night, were longer and tighter than usual.

CHAPTER THIRTY

Chris to the Rescue

$\varepsilon_{ex} = \dfrac{dQ_{ex}}{de} \cdot \dfrac{e}{Q_{ex}}; \ \varepsilon_{in} = \dfrac{dQ_{in}}{de} \cdot \dfrac{e}{Q_{in}}$

$NE(e) = Q_e(e) - eQ_{in}(e),$

$\Delta NE = \dfrac{dQ_{ex}}{de} \Delta e - e \dfrac{dQ_{in}}{de} \Delta e - eQ_{im} \cdot \ , (4)$

$B(a, b) = \displaystyle\int_0^1 (1-x)^{b-1} d\dfrac{x^a}{a} = \beta_{yx} = r \dfrac{1}{56}\left(7 + \sqrt{7\left(-5 + 4\sqrt{2}\right)}\right)\pi$

$= \dfrac{x^a(1-x)^{b-1}}{a}\Big|_0^1 + \dfrac{b-1}{a}\displaystyle\int_0^1 x^a(1-x)^{b-2}dx = \ f(x) = \dfrac{a_0}{2} + \sum_{n=1}^{\infty}(a_n\cos nx + b_n \sin n x)$

$= \dfrac{b-1}{a}\displaystyle\int_0^1 x^{a-1}(1-x)^{b-2}dx - \dfrac{b-1}{a}\displaystyle\int_0^1 x^{a-1}(1-x)^{b-1}dx =$

$= \dfrac{b-1}{a}B(a, b-1) - \dfrac{b-1}{a}B(a, b), \ r\left(\nabla x_f, \nabla y_f\right) = \dfrac{\sum_{i=1}^{N}\nabla x_f \cdot \nabla y_f}{\sqrt{\sum_{i=1}^{N}\nabla^2 x_f \cdot \sum_{j=1}^{N}\nabla^2 y_f}}$

$B(a, b) = \dfrac{b-1}{a+b-1}B(a, b-1) .= r_{yx} * \dfrac{S_y}{S_x}, \ (4)$

$-\displaystyle\iint \sqrt{x + \sqrt{y}}\ dx dy$

Integrate$[1/(x^6 + x^2 + 2)$

$\dfrac{8}{105}\left(x + \sqrt{y}\right)^{5/2}\left(-2x + 5\sqrt{y}\right)$

The Fall Semester classes were three quarters of the way through, and Beth was maintaining an 'A' average in every class. She worked hard to keep a high GPA. She was meticulously organized with her academic requirements. Her assignments were never late, and projects were intentionally designed to make sure the professors could see that she grasped the concepts being taught. All three-dimensional projects were colorful and well made. She was becoming particularly good at making fake trees out of bark.

With the exception of Intermediate Algebra, she didn't feel the classes were particularly challenging. Algebra class, however, didn't offer her the opportunity to improve her grade with "hands on" assignments, projects, and labs. It was simply quizzing, and tests. Math did not come easy for her, so this was to her disadvantage. Fortunately, she had an excellent professor, whose teaching methods suited her learning style, so she was able to maintain her 'A'. With three weeks left in the semester, Beth's Algebra teacher took a leave of absence and the position was filled with a young man who recently received his Doctorate in Mathematics. Beth didn't like him since the first class when he announced, "Things are going to change around here. I'm going to challenge you to become better students. I'll make you work hard to reach higher goals. I have strategies that will help you become more independent learners. As the end of the semester nears, the curriculum becomes naturally harder, so do my expectations."

As Beth prepared for her first quiz with the new professor, she began to feel the anxiety of an upcoming failure. She had never had a 'D', much less an 'F' before. Beth did the best she could to use the math book as her only source of reference, but as she finished a chapter, she felt more confused than when she had started. She needed a professor that could present the information in a more analogous way. She felt the new professor was not experienced or skilled enough to produce understandable logic. She told Anne he was pompous and trying to prove to himself that having his Doctorate somehow made him superior. He expected respect simply because he could put his new degree in front of his name. Most of the students in her class felt the same way, but that comradery wasn't going to change anything.

"Anne, I got an 'F' on my Algebra quiz!", Beth said over the phone almost crying. "I can't believe it! I never had an 'F' before! I don't know what to do. I hate this guy!"

"Okay Beth...try to relax. You're going to be okay. This is just one grade."

"Anne you don't get it. I'm lost. I don't understand any of these new chapters. I'm going to fail everything including the final exam! This guy doesn't teach us anything. He tells us the book was written by experts, and if we put in the effort, we'll do just fine. He's such an asshole!"

"We're going to figure this out. You're not going to fail."

"Yeah...maybe if I'm lucky, I'll get a 'D'."

"No, you're not…we'll find someone to tutor you. Isn't your roommate a math major?"

"Yes…but I can't ask her."

"Why?"

"I don't know. It would just feel weird."

"Do you want me to ask her for you?"

"No! That would feel even weirder."

"Well, then you have to do it yourself."

"Oh my God, this is going to be so hard. She thinks I'm smart and now she'll know I'm an idiot when it comes to math."

"No, she won't. Come on Beth…it will make her feel good."

Beth rambled on, "I don't even know how this guy got hired."

Anne concurred, "I've had really bad professors before too. I think they must do great in interviews because they give all the right answers, even though half of what they say isn't true. The ones who brag the most seem to be the ones who do the least. All they need to do is go back to the students they taught. They'll tell them the truth."

"Well…they obviously didn't ask any of his students," Beth said as she shook her head. "I'm not the only one who got an 'F' either. Half the class did, and I think he was proud of himself for it. Oh my God Anne…what am I going to do? You're a straight 'A' student, what would you do?"

"You're going to ask Chris for help, tonight. If you don't want me to do it, then you have to do it yourself and you can't wait. Do it tonight!"

"Chris can I talk to you?" Beth said.

"Sure."

"I have a new algebra teacher and I'm afraid I'm going to fail. He can't teach and almost everyone in class is lost. He doesn't teach us anything! He just tells us to use the book. I just can't seem to understand it no matter how hard I try." Beth paused for a moment before she got the courage to ask, "Is there any chance you can help me? I will pay you."

"Beth...you don't need to pay me. Of course, I will help you."

"Oh my God Chris...thank you, thank you, thank you. I promise to be a good student."

"I have no doubt you'll be. When do you want to start?"

Every evening after track practice, Chris sat with Beth for over an hour and presented the math in a way that made sense. Chris used repetition, rhymes, pictures, and analogies to help Beth understand it. It was like a pyramid. One concept was built on the other and Chris was giving Beth the solid foundation she needed. The results of the many practice quizzes Chris gave her, proved that Beth was grasping the concepts.

Beth understood that the time Chris devoted to Beth, came from time Chris generally used to complete her own academic responsibilities. Beth felt extremely guilty about this and continued to offer Chris money, but Chris adamantly refused to take it. A close bond began to develop between them. Beth saw Chris in a different light. She almost felt ashamed for not recognizing how caring and hardworking Chris was. Beth began to think the reason Chris had so many boyfriends was because she needed them to make her feel loved. Beth realized that Chris only presented herself as carefree, because she didn't have the confidence to let people know that she was truly a lovable, intelligent, and kind young woman. Obviously…no one in her life had helped her believe it.

"Well…how did you do?" Chris almost yelled at Beth when she entered their room holding the quiz in her hand."

"Take a look…" Beth said with a big smile as she handed her tutor the quiz.

"You got an 'A'! Oh my God…you did it Beth! Holy shit…you really did it!" Chris exclaimed with a smile that filled her face.

"And it was all because of you," Beth said placing a kiss on Chris's cheek. Chris blushed as a tear came to her eye.

CHAPTER THIRTY-ONE

Getting Caught

Beth's algebra grade was back up and both she and Anne held 'A' averages in all classes now. Their track records were equally excellent. As of yet, no one had beaten them, and they would not face their top rivals until after the winter break. They were looking forward to their much needed vacation.

Christmas break would be starting next weekend. Liza, who lived close, went home on Friday night to do some weekend Christmas shopping, and Michaela was going to be at a dance competition all day Saturday.

After a morning run, Anne and Beth went to Anne's apartment to shower and have lunch before they went to the Saturday Matinee at the movie theater in town. Beth had gotten in the habit of leaving extra clothing hidden in Anne's closet for occasions like this.

Beth showered first while Anne made lunch. Beth emerged from the bathroom in just her jeans and bra. She was about to put on her shirt when Anne came over and took it from her.

"You smell good," Anne said as she pulled Beth close to her and kissed her neck.

"You will too after you take a shower," Beth teased. Anne laughed as she pushed Beth down on the couch in the living room and laid on top of her. They both were laughing at first, but the laughter quickly changed to kissing.

"I'm home Anne! I got back early," Michaela called out as she opened the door.

Beth panicked. She knew she had no time to hide. She knew Michaela was standing by the door looking at them laying on the couch together. There was no other explanation for what she saw. They had been caught.

"I'm sorry…I didn't mean to interrupt you. I just came back to grab something and I'm heading right back out," Michaela said with a look of shock on her face. She didn't grab anything, she just hurried out without saying anything else.

"Oh my God Anne…" Beth said as she looked at Anne's frightened expression. Anne didn't say anything. Beth knew Anne's heart was racing as fast as hers.

"Oh shit…" Anne said as she sat up and shook her head. "I have no idea what I'm supposed to do now." Beth didn't have any suggestions either.

"Damn it! She wasn't supposed to be here! I can't even imagine what she's thinking," Anne said frustrated, "but I'm sure she's not fine with what she just saw."

"What are we going to do?" Beth asked nervously.

Anne thought for a moment before she said, "I have to tell her the truth. What else can I do. I don't want to live a lie anymore anyway. She either accepts us or she doesn't. I'll have to face her tonight and have an open discussion. Oh…I dread this."

"Do you want me to be with you?" Beth asked hoping Anne would say no.

"I would love your company, but I don't think that would help. I have to do this on my own. She's my roommate."

Beth and Anne went to the movies but neither of them seemed to be focused on the show. Anne drove Beth back to the dorm. Before Beth got out of the car, she leaned over and gave Anne a kiss. "Good luck tonight," Beth said softly.

Anne barely smiled, "I'll call you later and let you know what happened."

The conversation between Michaela and Anne never happened. Anne found out that Michaela had completed her academic responsibilities and decided to go home early. She left for home immediately after the dance competition.

Beth felt relieved when Anne told her that she wouldn't have to face Michaela until after the holiday break. She knew it would have to happen, but at least she wouldn't have to worry about it until after Christmas.

CHAPTER THIRTY-TWO

Christmas Gifts and Surprises!

Beth knew they wouldn't be together Christmas day, but they agreed they would make time to celebrate before they left for their homes. Beth started looking weeks ago, for a gift that would embody the deep and passionate love she felt for Anne. She decided that a wedding ring expressed this far better than anything else she could think of. A wedding ring would represent her commitment to their relationship and the permanence of her love.

Beth had been making payments on the ring that she wanted to the jewelry store in town. It was the most she could afford, and she knew Anne would appreciate the meaning more than the price. They would be going their separate ways on Saturday, so Beth was going to pick up the ring today. As Beth walked toward town, she could hear Christmas music coming from the old fire house loudspeaker. It was snowing lightly, and the streets looked like a blanket of white glitter. Christmas lights, ornaments and a variety of decorations lined the streets and filled store windows. Beth felt the spirit of the holiday. As she walked toward a large red Salvation Army pot, she pulled out her last dollar from her pocket. She crumpled it into a ball, and with one hand, shot it into the pot. "Basket," she whispered. The Santa Claus, who was standing next to the pot and ringing a large bell, smiled, and said," Merry Christmas honey…nice shot."

When Beth returned from the jewelry store, she wrapped the crushed velvet ring box in gold paper and put a red bow on it. She was eager to share a private Christmas with Anne. It reminded her of the euphoria she felt when she was a child. Her parents always made Christmas a magical time. The memory carried mixed emotions. She still missed her parents every day, especially this time of the year.

Chris came back to the room just after Beth finished wrapping the ring. Chris had a gift in her hand and presented it to Beth.

"Oh my gosh Chris…you didn't need to get me anything. Hold on though, I have something for you too," Beth said as she grabbed a small, wrapped box out of a drawer.

Chris spoke first, "I'm sorry I don't have the money to buy you the car you said you need, but I wanted to give you something to tell you how much I appreciate and care about you," Chris said sincerely.

"Well thank you," Beth blushed as she opened the neatly wrapped box to find a silver key chain with two charms hanging from it, a pair of miniature sneakers and a heart. Beth smiled, "Chris, thank you so much. Those sneakers may not fit, but that heart means the world to me." Beth gave Chris a warm hug.

Beth spoke next, "I want to tell you how much I've grown to appreciate and love you. You're really a very special person Chris. I'm glad I got to know you better." Beth felt like she might cry, so she relied on humor as a cover. "All right…open this before I start getting emotional," she said as she handed Chris her gift. I wish I could have afforded to buy you the new tires you said you needed for your convertible, but this will have to do. Chris opened her box to find another small box. Inside was a miniature replica of Chris's yellow convertible.

"I guess you can tell I had to paint it because it only came in red. It's the thought that counts though, isn't it?"

"Of course it is. Thank you, Beth," Chris said softly. "I'm really going to miss you."

"I'll miss you too," Beth said, "but I'll see you when you get back."

Chris stared at Beth for a moment before she spoke. Her eyes became watery, and her expression turned sorrowful. "I'm afraid you won't be seeing me after the break. I won't be coming back for the rest of the year," Chris said with a shaky voice.

"What?" Beth exclaimed. "Why?"

"I found out two days ago that I'm pregnant."

Beth was stunned. She didn't know what to say. She hesitated for a moment, then smiled and said sweetly, "Well...congratulations Chris. You're going to make a great mom!"

"Thank you for saying that Beth...I hope you're right," Chris said sadly.

"Are you okay? You seem upset," Beth said as she put her hand on Chris's shoulder.

"Well...this isn't exactly how I imagined my life would be right now. This definitely wasn't planned, but I can't blame anyone but myself. I just don't think I'm ready to be a mother yet," Chris said fighting back the tears.

"You'll be a great mother," Beth said smiling warmly.

"Oh well...I'm sure it will work out," Chris said as though she was trying to convince herself.

"It will Chris, don't worry," Beth said as she hugged her. "You'll figure it out. You just make sure you get your degree," Beth said as she stepped back and looked Chris directly in the eyes.

"I will, don't worry," Chris smiled.

"You better…we can't have a brilliant mind like yours go to waste!"

"Beth…I'm sorry we won't be roommates anymore, but I expect you to call me and let me know how you're doing."

"I will…I'll still miss you though. You can never be replaced," Beth said as she hugged Chris tight and whispered, "You just make sure you get that kid a good pair of sneakers."

CHAPTER THIRTY-THREE

Christmas at the Stetson's

It was about an hour before Anne was supposed to pick Beth up and take her back to her apartment for their private Christmas, when Beth's phone rang. It was Anne. "Beth," Anne said sounding upset, "I just got a call from my mom that my father is in the hospital. He had a heart attack."

"Oh my God Anne...I'm so sorry. How is he?"

"My mom told me she thinks he's going to be okay, but they need to do surgery right away." Anne's voice was shaky. Beth could tell she had been crying.

"Anne...I just know he's going to be okay. Don't worry."

"I'm so scared Beth...I don't want anything to happen to him. I have to leave right away. I'm sorry Beth, but I have to go now. We'll have to celebrate later. I feel horrible about this. I'm so sorry."

"Anne are you kidding...stop apologizing. Would you like me to come with you? I don't think you should drive by yourself. I'll drive you. I can call my brother, he would understand. I really want to go with you."

"Beth...I want you to come with me, but I don't want you to be away from your family. I feel terrible asking you to stay with me."

"Anne," Beth asserted, "pack your stuff and pick me up in an hour. I'll be ready." Beth called her brother, and he was completely supportive of her decision.

Beth drove Anne's car to the hospital. On the way there, Beth filled Anne in on Chris's pregnancy and Chris's decision not to finish the school year. Anne seemed as surprised and saddened as Beth was. They discussed the options regarding Beth getting another roommate, but neither of them knew the protocol. Beth kidded Anne about leaving her apartment and coming to live with her in the dorm. Beth was hoping she wouldn't be assigned another roommate, so she and Anne would have a place to be together, particularly after getting caught by Anne's roommate.

When they finally reached the hospital, Anne found her mother in the waiting room. She seemed as nervous as Anne, but you could see her relief when Anne went over and gave her a hug. Before she could fill Anne in on what was happening, the doctor came in and asked her mother if she was Mrs. Stetson. Her mother's face went as white as Anne's.

"All good news. We put in some stents and he'll be as good as new. We'll keep him overnight and send him home with you tomorrow. Everything's going to be all right, so enjoy your Christmas holidays!" the doctor said smiling.

When Mr. Stetson returned home it was as if nothing had ever happened. His energy was high and his face was always filled with a smile. It was five days until Christmas. Beth was considering borrowing Anne's car to go to her brothers. She figured she could come back and pick Anne up after the holiday. She didn't really want to, but she felt it might seem odd for her to stay when she really wasn't needed any more. She wasn't a part of their family and she didn't want to intrude on the Stetson's family traditions. When she mentioned the idea of leaving, Anne became upset, and Mr. and Mrs. Stetson insisted that she stay, unless of course, she wanted to be with her brother. They told her she was a welcomed part of their family. Beth decided to stay.

Life at the Stetson's seemed to return to normal after just a few days. Mr. Stetson made breakfast every morning and Mrs. Stetson kept everything running smoothly. The cold weather didn't stop Anne and Beth from taking their morning runs, but there was no skinny dipping in the pond. The sleeping arrangements were the same as Beth's first visit, and so were the intimate, rendezvouses late every night. Anne told Beth they had to make up for all the time they couldn't find privacy to have sex, and she seemed to have meant it. Somehow, they managed to muffle the sounds of their delight.

Anne's grandparents lived a few hours from the Stetson's home in a community near the ski slopes. It was customary for the grandparents to visit the day after Christmas. This year however, her grandparents were taking a cruise, and had arranged their visit after the new year.

It was three days before Christmas. The Stetson's home was already tastefully decorated inside and out, but there was still an empty spot in the living room, which was ready to be filled with a beautiful Christmas tree.

"All right everybody…it's time to go pick out our Christmas tree. This year I've decided Anne and Beth will take full responsibility. Beth, you and Anne will go out there," he said pointing to the woods surrounding the house, "and pick us a nice Douglas Fir, cut it down, and drag it back. We'll decorate it Christmas Eve."

Anne seemed excited. She smiled at Beth, "Do you feel up to it?"

"I guess so. Do we just go out into the woods with a saw and cut one down?

"Yup," Anne laughed. "It may seem old fashion but it's our tradition to have a huge tree that is fresh cut, and still has that wonderful Christmas tree smell."

"I know what smell you're talking about from when I was younger. We always had real trees back then. I love that smell! My brother, unfortunately, has fake ones. The only smell they have is like plastic," Beth laughed.

Go get your coat, we're going hunting for a tree," Anne said eagerly.

The air was cold, and the tree branches were spotted with white snow. Anne and Beth trudged through the woods, pointing out trees that were possibilities. Finally, they came upon one that they agreed would be perfect.

"This tree is gigantic," Beth said as she looked up at it. "Will it fit in the door?"

"We'll measure and cut some off the bottom when we get back. Are you ready to start sawing? I know my Dad keeps this hand saw blade sharp, just for this occasion."

Beth and Anne took turns cutting the thick trunk and cheered when it finally fell. They began pulling it back through the trees, laughing every time it got stuck on something. They sang Christmas songs and Anne laughed hysterically when Beth couldn't remember the words, so she would simply make up her own. Beth was giddy with happiness.

The fireplace in the living room flickered with warmth, and the hot chocolate in Beth's and Anne's hands was still steaming when Anne suddenly announced, "I have a great idea! We can drive to my grandparents tonight, stay over and go skiing tomorrow. I know where they keep the key and I'm sure they would love us to use their home. They have skis we can use too."

"I've never skied in my life," Beth laughed.

"Don't worry I can teach you. We'll use the beginner slopes to start. Come on let's do it! You've never backed away from a challenge before," Anne grinned.

It was sunset when they reached Anne's grandparent's home. The house was tucked away in the woods and looked like a storybook picture.

"This place is magical…I don't think I'm ever going to want to leave," Beth said grinning at Anne.

"Grab your stuff and get in here. It's too cold to stand outside and admire it," Anne teased. "Let's go in and get a fire going."

That evening was a perfect ending to a fairy-tale day. Their good night kisses would become an enchanted memory that Beth would cherish dearly. They fell asleep on the floor in front of the fireplace wrapped in blankets and each other.

"They seem to fit," Anne said as she helped Beth put on her skis.

"Don't laugh at me when I fall flat on my ass!" Beth laughed.

"I know you'll do just fine. Since when, haven't you been able to learn things quickly?"

"I have a feeling this might be an exception."

Anne guided Beth through the basics and thus far, Beth had shown quick success.

"I think we're ready for level two," Anne said as she took Beth to the lift for a steeper hill.

"Oh boy...that looks a little scary." Beth said making a face.

"We'll go at the same time. I'll be right by you, just like when we run. We can even finish together if you want," Anne said encouragingly.

"All right I'm ready," Beth said as she took a deep breath.

Beth stayed close to Anne as they descended. Her confidence was building, and she made no attempt to slow herself. Beth was enjoying the speed. Anne started to try to signal to Beth to slow down, but Beth didn't notice it. Beth was going straight down. Anne pulled alongside of Beth and was yelling something, but Beth was caught up in the thrill and couldn't hear her. When they were getting near the bottom, Beth began to lose control. Suddenly, she lost her balance and fell forward, causing her to bounce, then go flying up into the air, taking Anne down with her. They tumbled down the hill together, not slowing much until they reached the bottom.

"Are you all right!" Beth yelled to Anne in a panic as she stood up. She knew it was her fault and she would never be able to forgive herself if Anne were hurt.

Anne was wiping the snow off her face and laughing hard, "Oh my God Beth…we don't always have to finish side by side."

Beth started laughing uncontrollably, "Did we win?"

Christmas Eve at the Stetson's was like a dream. The holiday music played while they ate warm fresh Christmas cookies and drank Eggnog with just a tad of liquor in it. The tree was filled with ornaments that carried many memories for Anne. Some were homemade and given to her by friends or family members. One of Anne's favorites was the one she made for her mom in second grade. It was made from a popsicle stick and glitter.

When the tree was lit and the tinsel was sparkling, Beth caught a glimpse of Anne staring at the tree. She looked absolutely beautiful. That angel, Beth thought, is the greatest gift I will ever receive.

After everyone kissed goodnight, Beth and Anne went to their rooms until Anne's parents went to bed and turned off their light. Beth waited impatiently for Anne to open the door and sneak in. Beth had the ring under her pillow. Finally, the door squeaked open and Anne hurried in and slipped under the warm covers next to Beth.

"Merry Christmas," Anne said as she kissed Beth on the lips. "It's after midnight so I can officially say that."

"Merry Christmas my gorgeous elf," Beth said as she returned the kisses. "Anne, I can't believe I'm lying here with you on Christmas Eve. I think I must be dreaming. If I don't tell you enough already, I want you to know how much I love you, and how happy you've made me. I didn't think I could ever be this happy again."

"I feel the same way. We're truly blessed. I think our guardian angels are watching over us more than we realize. They brought us together, I'm sure of that."

"Then this is what heaven must feel like," Beth said as she stared into Anne's eyes.

"Let's never forget this moment..." Anne said as she kissed Beth's soft lips.

"I have something for you Anne," Beth said as she pulled her gift from under the pillow. "Since it's after midnight you may open it."

"I have something for you too..." Anne said as she hung off the side of the bed and pulled a small gift from underneath. "I had to sneak in here earlier today to hide it from you."

"All right...on the count of three we'll open them at the same time. "One, two, three." They opened their small boxes slowly, occasionally looking up at each other to make sure they weren't going too fast. Beth took the bow and paper off and saw a box similar to the one she had given Anne. Anne finished at the same time and looked up at Beth. They both looked at each other and laughed.

"You go first," Beth tried to insist.

"No, we'll open them at the same time. Ready, go."

Beth opened her velvet box and found a stunning gold ring, embedded with small diamonds, glittering back at her. It was remarkably similar to the one she bought Anne. Beth's heart pounded with love and excitement upon seeing it.

Anne opened her box at the same time. She pulled out the gold and diamond ring that Beth had chosen, to represent her forever lasting love for Anne.

"This is beautiful…I love it," they said at exactly the same time. They admired their rings quietly for a moment. Beth felt emotional just looking at hers. She spoke softly as she told Anne, "Someday we'll be able to say, 'Will you marry me?' to go along with these rings."

"Well, no one is stopping us right now…so what do you say Beth Locke? Will you give your heart to me forever and join me in marriage?"

"Yes, of course…and Anne Stetson, will you love me forever come richer or poorer…even if I'm wearing a Ranger hat?"

"Of course, I will. Hat or no hat, I'll love you forever."

They slid their rings on each other's ring finger and sealed their love with a kiss and a night of intimacy.

CHAPTER THIRTY-FOUR

Welcome Back

Beth felt a touch of sadness when Anne dropped her off at the dorm. She was having to force herself to wake up from her idyllic Christmas dream. The new year was about to begin.

Beth was afraid to see what her room looked like without Chris's presence. She slowly opened her door and peaked in. It seemed barren. Every sign that Chris had once lived there was gone. It felt empty and lonely. She missed Chris already.

Anne entered her apartment and threw her bags down by the door. Something was different. All of Michaela's belongings were gone. Michaela had moved out.

"Welcome home Anne," Liza called out from the kitchen.

"Hey Liza…am I cracking up or did someone steal all of Michaela's belongings?" Anne asked in confusion.

"Come sit down…" Liza said as she walked from the kitchen into the living room and pointed to the couch. It happened to be the same couch that Michaela had caught Anne and Beth making out on. "First of all, did you have a nice Christmas?" Liza smiled.

"Yes, I did…it was perfect. Now, are you going to tell me what's going on?"

"Well…I got a call from Michaela over the break. She told me about walking in on you and Beth."

"Oh shit…I knew it."

"No, no. She wasn't that upset over it. She and I had suspected it anyway."

"Oh my God…I can't believe this is happening,"

"Don't worry, we didn't talk that much about it behind your back."

"Oh, that makes me feel better…" Anne said sarcastically.

"I'm sure she wasn't thrilled that you brought Beth over and used the couch to have a make out session, but she wasn't judging your lifestyle. She just said she felt like she was ready to have a place of her own."

"She never mentioned that before," Anne said uncomfortably.

"I was a little surprised…but I get it. I think she's feeling that it's time for her to become a 'real grown up'. You and I both know she's a lot more mature than we are." Anne smiled in agreement.

"I have a feeling that catching you guys wasn't the cause, it was just the final kick in the ass she needed to make a decision." Anne put her head between her hands.

"Anne…don't let it upset you. She still loves you," Liza said smiling and putting her arm around Anne's shoulder.

"I don't even know what to say," Anne said shaking her head.

"Don't say anything. It's not that big a deal. Michaela is my best friend and I'm not worried, so you shouldn't be either. Things change…just go with the flow."

Anne was still in shock and trying to process everything.

"Hey Anne…I'm an art major. You must have figured out that half of the guy friends I have are gay."

"Actually no…I never even thought about it!"

"Well, they are. Steven is my 'real' boyfriend, but the rest are the gay guys that I hang out with. Michaela knows about it. She hasn't said anything negative. Think about it...she does ballet. Three quarters of her male dance partners are probably gay. As a matter of fact, I think it's time you and Beth get to know some of my gay friends. You'll absolutely love them."

Anne called Beth as soon as she was able to pull herself out of her fog. She still couldn't believe this was happening. "Beth, you're not going to believe this..."

Anne filled Beth in on the several surprises that awaited her when she had returned home and entered her apartment. Beth was shaken at first, but Anne calmed her by sharing Liza's point of view. Anne reassured Beth that they just needed to look for the silver lining. It would expose itself, they just needed to be patient. Anne was right. Since losing their roommates, Beth and Anne had more opportunities for privacy. Life seemed less complicated. Balancing academics, sports, and their love life, was much simpler. Beth was happy and temporarily content with the living arrangements. Someday, she was convinced, they would have a place of their own.

CHAPTER THIRTY-FIVE

Meeting the Boys

The invitational meets were done for now, and the upcoming schedule included only teams within their division. The first two meets were against teams they had competed against in the pre-season. The races were extremely close, but the results were the same. Beth and Anne were still undefeated in the Division and Carol finished third in both.

After Friday's meet, Anne spoke with Carol, Mia, and Abby, and extended an invitation to get together with her and Beth on Saturday night. Anne said she would plan something and give them a call. Without hesitation, they all accepted the invitation.

Anne had grown closer to her roommate Liza. She was comfortable asking Liza if she would mind if she invited some of her girlfriends over for a small party. She also wanted to know if Liza would join them. Liza seemed thrilled that Anne extended the invitation and offered to call some of her "gay guy" friends. Anne and Beth were thrilled with the idea of meeting other gay people.

Anne called Carol first to make sure everything would be okay with that. Carol said she was looking forward to it and asked if it would be okay to invite Lex. Anne couldn't hold back a smile as she told Carol that Lex was more than welcome to join them. Next Anne called Abby and Mia.

"All right...here's the plan," Anne said as soon as Mia answered the phone, "We'll meet at my apartment at eight o'clock tomorrow night. If it's okay with you, Liza's going to invite some of her gay guy friends over too. What do you say? Are you in?"

"Absolutely," Mia said eagerly, "but I want to ask you…do you mind if I invite my brother?"

"Of course, I don't mind, but why do I feel there's a story behind this?" Anne kidded.

"Believe it or not, over the holidays, I came out to my brother, who by the way is my twin, and he told me he was gay too."

"Oh my God…are you kidding?"

"I know, can you believe it?" Mia said laughing.

"Do your parents know?"

"I'll let him fill you in tomorrow night. You don't mind if he brings a friend, do you?"

"No, that would be great. I have a feeling this is going to be a very interesting party."

Liza and Anne's apartment filled quickly. Liza's boyfriend, Steven, who now stayed over at the apartment as frequently as Beth did, had already tapped the keg and made sure everyone had an ice cold mug. Five of Liza's gay friends came in just after the girls. Liza made the introductions, and it was only a short period of time before everyone was engaged in conversation.

"When is your brother coming, Mia?" Anne asked.

"He is picking up his boyfriend and should be here shortly."

"I can't wait to meet him. Is he as talented and attractive as you?"

"Of course, he is…" Mia joked.

"Someone's here." Liza's friend Jeffery yelled as he jumped up and answered the door. "Well please do come in...I sincerely hope you're at the right place," Jeffery grinned as he welcomed the two men into the party. Mia got up and greeted her brother at the door.

"Everyone...this is my twin brother Michael, and his boyfriend Anthony," Mia said proudly.

"Hi everyone," Michael and Anthony said simultaneously. Jeffery leaned towards Beth and said under his breath, "They're freaking gorgeous! They must be models!"

"Oh my God, I think you might be right," Beth whispered. Michael and Anthony defined "tall, dark, and handsome", but Anthony's skin was darker, due to his African American and Spanish background.

"Can I get you guys anything?" Liza asked.

"I think both of us could use a cold beer," Anthony said in his deep voice. Jeffery jumped at the opportunity and went and got them some beer. When he handed them the mugs, Jeffery introduced himself as Liza's best friend. Michael and Anthony expressed sincere gratitude for his hospitality, then quickly engaged him in conversation that was filled with frequent laughter.

After a few minutes, Mia waved Michael and Anthony over to join her. "Come over here and sit with us. I want to introduce you to the two girls I was telling you about."

"Oh, you mean the two cute runners you were bragging about?" Michael teased.

"Well...they are cute, aren't they?" Mia said as she smiled at Beth and Anne.

"Hey…what about me?" Abby joked. "What did you tell Michael about me?"

"Believe me…she never stops talking about you," Michael smiled.

"Michael, do you mind telling these guys the story about you and Anthony?" I already told them that I came out to you over the holiday." It took less than a minute for Michael to have a full audience.

Mia continued, "I just want everyone to know that I had no idea he was gay. He has always been the perfect son. He's been polite, smart, super athletic, and has finally turned out to be very handsome." Mia pinched Michael's cheek and smiled.

"I don't know if that's the truth but thank you anyway. Except for the handsome part, I can say the same about you. You were more popular though. Now that I think about it…you did have an awful lot of girlfriends," Michael said raising his eyebrows.

"Well so did you…you had girls hanging all over you. You always had a girlfriend."

"I do like women…but I found out that I like men more," Michael said as he smiled at Anthony.

Beth asked bashfully, "Is Anthony the first guy you've been with?"

"Yes, he is, but Anthony can't say the same." Anthony laughed.

"Where'd you meet?" Anne asked.

"I'm sorry if you think this is going to be some sort of steamy locker room story, but it's not. Believe it or not, we met through track. Just like all of you girls. There must be something about it."

"I think it's the short shorts and tight sleeveless tops," Abby kidded. Everyone laughed.

"Anyway…Anthony was a sprinter, and I did hurdles. We saw each other every day and started to talk more frequently. Anthony definitely didn't look or act gay, but I just had this weird feeling. Maybe it was the way he looked at me."

"How could I not want to look at you?" Anthony interjected.

"I felt myself becoming attracted to him. Maybe it was there all along, but I think I was fighting it. Finally, I asked him if he wanted to go get something to eat after practice, and the next thing I know we're sitting at McDonalds having dinner."

"That's a great first date," Jeffery kidded.

"It turned out to be," Anthony grinned.

"It was confusing though. I had absolutely no idea how to handle my feelings. I started thinking that if I say something to him about my feelings, he might kill me. How could I be sure he felt the same way. I was hoping he would say something first…and he did." Michael grinned at Anthony.

Anthony took over the story, "I had been with guys before. No one knew about it though, especially my parents. The few guys I had been with had already graduated and went to other schools. I met them in the gay bars in the city. I started going there when I was a junior. I'm tall so they thought I was older. I went by myself the first time. I was scared shitless…but it was worth it. I felt like I could be myself. I finally felt happy."

"I'm sure all the men at the bars were happy too," Jeffery interjected.

"I have a better radar than Michael. I had a gut feeling there might be a mutual attraction, so I decided to be completely honest. I told him I was gay and that I was attracted to him."

Michael jumped in, "And...I was a complete asshole and chickened out. I told him that it was cool, but I wasn't gay. He told me that he was sorry if he misinterpreted anything and being friends was good enough. He did, however, give me his number and say that if I ever changed my mind or just wanted to talk outside of track practice, to call him. It only took me a week...but I finally called him. The rest is history.

"What was the second date?" Jeffery asked.

"Pizza Hut...and I paid," Michael laughed.

Liza asked a question that Beth was thinking about. "Anthony, do your parents know?"

"No...I want to tell them so badly because they are such wonderful people. I'm afraid to embarrass them in front of their friends. It doesn't always go over to well in the black and Hispanic communities," Anthony said disappointedly. "I hope to someday though. I know they just want me to be happy, and I want them to see that I am extremely happy. Someday things may change, but for right now it's our little secret," Anthony said pausing before he added, "I guess it's not much of a secret anymore since we just confessed to all of you." Everyone laughed, and Liza said, "I'm so glad you guys came and shared your story. It helps everyone when others are honest about who they are. Do your parents know that their perfect twins are gay?"

"No," Michael said quickly. "Their perfect little Jewish boy in love with a non-Jewish, African American, Hispanic man will be a little too much for them to handle."

Mia jumped in, "Maybe for Dad, but I think Mom would still love you. Telling them that both of their kids are gay might cause a little family trauma. Mom would be convinced that there's some kind of horrific genetic disorder in our family, and she would blame herself."

Michael tried to add some hope, "Don't worry, things will change someday. They'll have to. There's too many of us!"

The party continued and people shared their coming out stories. Some of the guys shared the physical abuse and bullying they experienced in high school. Jeffery's story was the most gut wrenching. He timidly shared that he had been raped on several occasions when he was seventeen, by two adult men that lived in his neighborhood. They were going to teach him a lesson, they said. They threatened to kill him if he told anyone. The threat didn't matter anyway…there was no one in his life that he would even consider telling. Until now, Jeffery had never shared this story with anyone but Liza.

The drinking, laughing, and development of friendships continued through the evening. The mood was that of validation and belonging. It was an evening that no one would forget.

"There was a knock at the door. Anthony jumped up, "Oh…that might be a good friend of mine that Mia said I could invite."

"I'll get it!" Jeffery yelled as he jumped up then opened the door to let another tall, dark, and handsome man into the party.

Anthony followed Jeffery to the door to introduce his friend, "I would like you to meet a close friend of mine," Anthony announced, "Everyone...this is Marco...Marco Diaz."

CHAPTER THIRTY-SIX

The Flu

Around noon, Beth got a call from Anne. "Beth…I have bad news for you." Anne sounded miserable.

"What's wrong?" Beth asked alarmed.

"I'm sick. I have the flu. I have a hundred- and two-degree temperature. I didn't go to any classes this morning because I've been throwing up."

"What? Why didn't you call me? I would have cut my classes and come over."

"That's why I didn't call you."

"I'm coming over now," Beth insisted.

"No…you're not. We have one of our biggest meets this afternoon and you will go," Anne said emphasizing the word "will".

"I don't care about the meet. I'm coming over to take care of you."

"No, you're not! You're going to run and you're going to have to win for me."

"Oh God Anne…I hate this. You're sick and I'm going to be sick if I even think about running without you."

"You can do it Beth. I'm sorry I can't talk about it anymore. I need to go lay down or I'm going to be sick again. I already called Coach Ryan so just go and win it for us. I love you," Anne said before she hung up.

Beth saw Carol stretching by the track. "Carol, Anne's not coming. She has the flu," Beth said anxiously.

"What? We're running against State! We need her!"

"She's really sick. She's been throwing up all morning."

"Oh my gosh…this really sucks," Carol said frustrated. After a moment of pensiveness, Carol came

288

around. "Beth...we're just going to have to do it without her." Beth nodded, "You know she'll kill us if we don't beat them."

"I know...we just need to stay ahead of those two girls, Brittany and Trish. We can do it. There's no reason we can't."

"I agree...no excuses. Anne wouldn't listen to them anyway."

"Come on Beth," Carol said with confidence, wrapping her arm around Beth's shoulder. "Let's just run our race. We'll beat them, don't worry about it. We're better than they are. Don't let them psych us out."

Beth grinned at Carol, "You're right. Nobody can control the way we think, but us. Let's make it happen."

As the runners approached the starting line, Beth heard a familiar voice taunting her from the stands. She tried hard to ignore it, but she found it personally offensive.

When the gun went off, Carol, Beth, and the State College top runners, Brittany, Trish, and two other new girls, stayed even with them. The race was shoulder to shoulder for three and a half laps. There was more bumping than usual. Beth was convinced that Brittany was doing it on purpose, but this only motivated her. As they came down the final stretch, Beth was just slightly behind the other five. She felt her anger beginning to stir. She was infuriated that she couldn't live up to Anne's expectations. She wasn't going to let this happen. She gave it everything.

Photo finish results confirmed that Beth took first and Carol second. Beth was elated with the win, but still angry about the body contact that happened on the track.

"I'm going to say something to them about trying to knock us off our step," Beth told Carol.

"I can't tell you what to do...but I'm not joining you," Carol said. "I'm used to it."

Beth walked up to Trish and Brittany who were standing nearby.

"Why did you feel the need to bump us around? Are you afraid you couldn't beat us fair and square?" Beth said looking directly at Brittany. A woman sitting on the bleachers called out, "Brittany, don't waste your time having a conversation with her. She's a cheater!" Brittany ignored the woman. She just stared at Beth for a moment. There was no expression on her face. She spoke with a calm voice and never took her eyes off of Beth. "I will give you the benefit of being an inexperienced runner, but I will only tell you this once..." Beth was taken back. She expected a more defensive response.

"I have never cheated to win anything, and I doubt that will ever change." Then without changing her expression or tone, she added, "You ran a good race Beth. Congratulations on your win." Brittany extended her hand. Beth shook it and tried to think of something to say. She suddenly felt foolish.

"Thanks...I'm sorry. You ran a good race too."

Carol was standing by the side of the track waiting for Beth. "Well...did you get everything worked out?" she said smiling at Beth.

"Okay...I feel really stupid. I'm not usually like that. I don't know what's getting into me."

"Don't worry about it, you're still young." Carol said smiling as she gently punched Beth's shoulder.

"Why does everybody punch me?" Beth laughed rubbing her shoulder.

"Just because you're so damn cute. Now let's call Anne and give her the good news!"

"Okay...do you mind not telling Anne how I made an ass out of myself."

"Your secret is safe with me..."

As soon as they could, Carol and Beth called Anne together.

"We did it!" Carol and Beth yelled into the phone at the same time.

"You beat them? I knew you would! I'm so proud of you guys!"

"Oh...and your little shadow here beat me," Carol said laughing.

"You bet I did," Beth said grinning at Carol.

Anne just laughed, "I love you guys."

CHAPTER THIRTY-SEVEN

Cheer Squad

There would be one more meet before the Divisional Championship. Practices were challenging and critical. Even though Anne had missed the last meet, she, Beth, and Carol, were still unbeaten by any competitors on the indoor track. All of their times were well below the five-minute mark and still dropping.

On the day of the meet, Liza invited everyone from the party, who weren't competing themselves, to join her private cheering section. Her newly formed entourage began to cheer loudly as soon as they saw the girls enter the stadium. Beth, Anne, Carol, Mia, and Abby noticed them right away.

"I can't believe you guys came!" Anne called out as she walked towards them.

"We're your new cheer squad, so get over here and let us give y'all some big, good luck hugs and kisses," Jeffrey yelled back. Sincere smiles and hugs were exchanged.

"Michael, what are you and Anthony doing here? You should be at your own track practice." Mia asked.

"I couldn't miss my sister compete, so Anthony and I are playing hooky."

"Ahhh…that's sweet, now I guess I have to come watch you guys compete too."

Liza, acting as the social director, said her group would watch Mia and Abby in the relay first, then all of them would come to watch the women's mile.

"Us boys have to find some time to watch Marco too. I want to see him without all that clothing on," Jeffery kidded.

"Don't worry, you'll have time to watch his dark, powerful legs, go pumping by," Anne smirked.

"Yeah...that's not all I'd like to see pumping..." Everyone laughed.

Beth was excited, "I can't believe you guys came. This is so cool. I guess we better win now! Hey, do you think you could come on Monday and watch us in the Divisional Championship? We plan on taking it all...we'll make you proud," Beth grinned.

"We wouldn't miss it for the world!" Michael said.

"I'll bring the cheering squad again. We're our own little team now so we'll be there for you," Liza said, wrapping her arm over the shoulders of Jeffery and Anthony, sitting next to her.

"All right...thanks guys! Our coach wants us, so we'll catch up later." Anne waved goodbye as she and the other girls started jogging towards Coach Ryan.

"Well...this is our last meet before the Divisional Championship," Coach Ryan said to the group of runners she had pulled aside. "I can't tell you how proud I am of all of you. I don't think I've ever had a group of girls who worked so hard. Some of you were even willing to push yourself to the point of collapsing," Coach said as she looked at Beth. "Yeah...I mean you, Beth Locke with an E." Beth smiled while the others laughed. "Some of you took on the leadership roles that are necessary to become a winning team, and we truly are a team. I can say the same about our field event athletes too, but there is something special about this group. I can feel the love between you. I know how much you care for each other. Please don't lose that. No matter what happens to you, that bond will help you get through the hard times. Now let's go run our races with determination and confidence. I have no doubt we'll show them what it means to be a champion."

Coach Ryan was right…they took the top three spots.

Anne finished first in every meet in the indoor season, and Beth and Carol had never been defeated by an opponent. They were true champions, and they couldn't wait for the Divisional Championship to start on Monday, so they could prove it to everyone.

CHAPTER THIRTY-EIGHT

The Phone Call

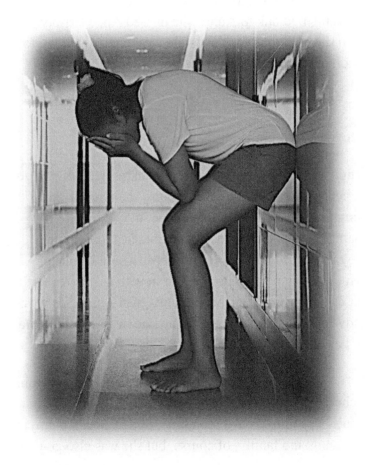

Anne left Friday night to join her parents for a family gathering. Beth got up early Saturday morning for a quick run and then spent the rest of the day catching up on schoolwork. She had invitations to join others on Saturday night, but chose to stay back so she could have the privacy she wanted, to talk to Anne. She missed Anne terribly when she was gone for the whole weekend but talking to her on the phone, helped Beth feel less lonely.

Saturday 7:00 p.m.

Beth's phone rang at seven o'clock sharp. Beth always got excited when the phone rang because she knew it was going to be Anne. They talked about the Regional Championships on Monday and strategies for winning. They were absolutely sure the winner would be one of them. They came up with ideas of how to celebrate later that evening. Beth was more excited than Anne. She was ready for this one. Nothing and no one, was going to hold her back.

Before they hung up, Beth told Anne she was going to church on Sunday to pray. She was raised Catholic but hadn't been to mass in a long time. She planned on praying for friends and family, of course, but she was also going to ask God to help them perform their best at Regionals. Perhaps that was a bit selfish, but she didn't use the word "win." Beth felt that made it more acceptable in God's eyes.

Sunday 9:00 a.m.

Sunday was a beautiful day. It was warm and sunny, and painted with a rich blue sky, void of clouds. Beth decided to go for a short run on the cross-country course before she started her schoolwork. Beth knew Anne would be back by eight o'clock tonight, and she wanted to be caught up on all of her work before she got there. She could almost feel the welcome back kisses they would share.

Sunday 7:00 p.m.

The phone rang around seven o'clock. Beth figured it was Anne calling to tell her she would be there soon.

"Hello," Beth said as she smiled in anticipation of hearing Anne's voice.

"Hello, Beth Locke?"

"Yes." She didn't recognize the voice.

"This is Janice Amway," the voice was low and serious. "I'm Anne's Aunt." Beth was as much disappointed, as she was confused. She had never met her.

"I'm sorry, but Anne isn't here."

"Yes, I know," the woman said quietly. "It is you I want to talk to. Anne's mother asked me to call…" Beth nervously waited for an explanation.

299

"Beth... I'm afraid I have some bad news for you..." Beth's stomach knotted up. Thoughts flashed through her mind.

"It's about Anne..." Beth's heart stopped. That was exactly what she feared hearing the most.

"What? What happened to her?" Beth's mind exploded with fear.

There was a pause, "Anne was in a very serious car accident."

"Oh my God..." Beth's voice was shaking.

"Beth, I'm sorry but..." Beth's heart stopped cold. She didn't want to hear the rest.

"Anne didn't make it...she died. Beth, I'm so deeply sorry." Beth was silent.

The woman continued, "They said it happened instantly, so at least Anne shouldn't have felt any pain." Beth stood motionless with the phone to her ear.

"There will be a private gathering at four o'clock tomorrow. Anne's family would like you to be there to discuss the arrangements for her funeral. They said you were special to her and her dearest friend." Beth's body was trembling.

"I'm sorry I had to bring you this terrible news. I know how much this must hurt you." No...she would never know the pain Beth was feeling.

Beth hung up without saying a word. She couldn't speak, nothing would come out. This had to be a mistake, some error, and once discovered, would bring Anne back to her. It had to be. It was a nightmare and she just had to wake herself up. She threw the phone across the room and watched it break apart. It was how she felt...completely broken. She put her head in her hands as she slid down the wall. Her face lost all color. She felt she couldn't breathe. Nothing seemed real. Her eyes were empty as she stared at nothing. Her body started shaking uncontrollably. Words started spilling out of her mouth as she begged,

"No...no...no...NO!!! Please God...please God, make this not true! Please God don't do this...PLEASE GOD, PLEASE NO!" Tears were streaming down her face. She couldn't feel them because she was numb. Her mind was in shock and her heart filled with agony...a pain so deep that she couldn't bear it.

"Why Anne? You can't do this! Please, I'll do anything. Please God! PLEASE GOD!" she cried out. "Take me, please take me...I don't want to live without her. I can't live without her." She was sobbing so hard she was having trouble catching her breath. Her sobbing continued uncontrollably as her body shook. She was weak from the unbearable pain. Her love for Anne was deep and consuming. Anne was her life. She brought her such happiness. Anne was the reason she wanted to live. There was no reason now…

Beth couldn't tolerate the anguish and emptiness. She didn't want to live in this world without her. She needed to join Anne.

Beth knew that Stevie, the girl who lived in the room next door, had a small pocket pistol. Her father, a police officer, said he would feel better if she had one. She usually carried it in her purse when she went out. Sometimes she kept it in her desk drawer though. If I'm lucky, Beth thought, it will be there. She knocked…no answer. She entered the room and opened the drawer…it was there. Beth took the gun back to her room and sat down on her bed. Her hand was shaking so hard she had trouble holding it. But it wasn't from fear, it was from the anguish. She wasn't afraid. This would be easy. She would feel badly for her brother, but he would have to understand that she had no other choice. She couldn't handle the agony of losing Anne. Beth got a pen and a piece of paper and wrote him a note.

"My dear brother Dave, I'm sorry if I hurt you because you have been my hero. Please understand that I need to be with Anne. I have no other choice. I love you forever."

Beth sat down on the floor and put her back against the wall. She placed towels all around her and over her shoulders, so there would be less to clean up. She decided the best place would be her temple, so she raised the gun and pressed it tightly against it. She took a deep breath. "I'm coming Anne...please don't be mad. I know there is a heaven and I know I will be with you and my parents. We'll be happy for eternity. It all makes sense. I love you too much to live without you," Beth sobbed uncontrollably.

With her hand still shaking, Beth closed her eyes, took a deep breath...and pulled the trigger.

CHAPTER THIRTY-NINE

Where Are You Beth?

Sunday 7:40 p.m.

Anne had to call Beth later than normal because she was held up by talkative relatives and didn't want to be rude. It was about seven forty when she finally got a chance to call. Anne let the phone ring but there was no answer. The answering machine picked up,

"Hey... my little angel. Where are you? I got the call from the athletic director's secretary about the meet being canceled tomorrow, so I'm going to stay another night. I miss you so much I can't stand it. I'll call you in an hour. I can't wait to talk to you. I love you forever..."

Sunday 8:30 p.m.

"Hey Beth, it's eight thirty and I'm checking in. I don't know where you are but I'm hoping you're out having a good time without me, by the way. As soon as you get this message please call me."

Sunday 10:00 p.m.

"All right Beth...now I know you're out having a good time. It's ten o'clock and I'm heading to bed, so if you get in soon, call me. I should call you nice and early in the morning to make sure you pay for the hangover, but I'll be nice, I'll let you call me when it's convenient. I'm glad we don't have classes tomorrow. I'll stop by on my way back to the apartment. God I can't believe how much I miss you and looking forward to our kisses. You're more important to me than anything. Never forget that. I'll love you forever."

CHAPTER FORTY

Promises Made

"Fuck!!!" Beth yelled when the gun didn't fire. It must have been an empty chamber. She knew Stevie usually kept bullets in it. She saw her put them in once. She put the gun back up to her head. Her hand twitched, she had one last chance to change her mind, but she didn't. This time she heard the click as she pulled the trigger.

"God Damn it!!!" She cried when the gun didn't go off again. "Anne…help me, help me get through this please…" she begged. Beth had committed herself to ending her life. She desperately needed to find those bullets. She went back to Stevie's room and pulled the desk drawer back open. No luck. She started going through other drawers. She looked under the bed, in closets, in shoe boxes. She found nothing. She needed to end her pain and be with Anne. She had to find another way.

Beth returned to her room. She was frantic and completely lost. She felt like she was outside of her body, watching a horrible movie. She just wanted to escape from it all.

Beth hurriedly put on her sneakers and ran from her room, through the lobby and into the drizzling dark night. The air felt heavy and cold. She began running quickly, picking up speed as she headed to her final destination…the cross-country course. The place where she first met Anne. There was a spot at the peak of the highest hill where large rocks hung over a steep cliff. Reaching that spot was her goal. She had little light as she began to ascend the steepest hill. Her pace was frantic and desperate, mirroring her feelings.

It was raining harder now, and the course was dark and very slippery. She could barely stay on the path. She slipped and fell several times. Each time she willed herself up and continued running with more desperation. She ran blindly into tree branches, leaving welts and scratches everywhere on her body. Her breathing turned into gasps. She fell hard, tripping over a hidden rock. She got up to her knees and grabbed a handful of mud and threw it as hard as she could into the rainy darkness. "Damn you Anne! Why did you leave me!!!" she yelled as loud as she could. She began sobbing and could barely breathe. Her body was covered with mud. Her knees were bloody, and a mixture of rain and tears rolled off her face. She was devastated and couldn't imagine living without Anne.

She was almost to the top. She could see the silhouette of the bolder that hung out over the cliff. Just a few more steps would bring her relief.

Beth moved closer to the edge. She tried to stand motionless, but her body was shaking, and her chest was rising and falling rapidly as her lungs struggled to get enough air. She looked down. It would work. She knew it would. She made her apologies to Anne, God, and her family. She took several deep breaths and started to take the two steps she needed to begin the end…but she couldn't move. Her legs were frozen. She wasn't afraid, but something was stopping her. Her thoughts became fuzzy, things weren't as clear as they were just moments before. "Anne," Beth said crying, "if you're up there, please talk to me. I promise I'll do whatever you want me to do."

Suddenly a vivid memory overwhelmed her. She envisioned Anne sitting there on the bathroom floor in the stadium. Her beautiful face was filled with a warm smile and she was sticking her pinkie out and hooking it around Beth's. She was making Beth promise that no matter what, if she couldn't finish a race, Beth would have to finish on her behalf. Beth dropped to her knees and sobbed. She never broke promises...she said that to Anne many times. How could she keep this promise when she had to meet with Anne's parents to plan Anne's funeral?

"Please Anne...just tell me what to do," Beth sobbed. "What am I supposed to do...please just tell me," Beth pleaded, her face in her hands and weeping uncontrollably.

By the time Beth had no more tears to shed, and her body was utterly exhausted, she had made the decision. For the sake of Anne's parents, she would go help plan the funeral tomorrow and would have to run for Anne at some other time. She knew she would miss the divisional championship, but she had no choice. She wouldn't promise anyone though, that she wouldn't, at some other time, end her life. Beth got to her feet and began the descent down the hill in the cold, rainy, darkness.

Beth opened the door to her room. She was covered in mud and blood, but no one saw her. She didn't care anyway. She didn't care about anything. She was still in shock and had no recollection of how she got back to her room. It was past eleven o'clock. She laid down on her bed. She didn't change out of her clothing. She stared up at the ceiling cursing God. She still hoped this was a nightmare, and if she could just fall asleep, she might wake up to find that none of this was real.

After a long, agonizing night, Beth finally cried herself to sleep. She fell briefly into a deep sleep and woke up in the late morning. She rubbed her puffy eyes and felt the sun coming in through the window. She forgot for a brief moment what had happened. Then the woman's voice from the phone call came flooding back. "Anne didn't make it…she's dead." The words kept repeating in her head. Each repetition was torture. She felt paralyzed from grief. Her body was frozen as she lay there staring up at the ceiling. She knew she had to get up to go meet the Stetsons, but she just couldn't seem to do that. Finally, she forced herself into the shower. She scrubbed herself so hard that the cuts began bleeding again. She wanted it to hurt. She wanted the pain to replace her unbearable heartache.

Beth made plans to borrow a car. She knew it was going to be a long drive. It was going to be the worst journey she'd ever take.

Beth decided she would tell no one about Anne's death before she left. What good would it do? She didn't want anyone to have to feel the anguish it would cause. Anne wouldn't want her to anyway.

As Beth dressed, she thought how absolutely dreadful and heart wrenching planning Anne's funeral was going to be. She feared seeing the devastation in Anne's parent's eyes. They will still be in shock, and like her, they won't be able to wake themselves from this cruel nightmare. Then they will have to have a viewing and funeral. People will be crying, and some will be asking why such a beautiful young woman didn't have a nice boyfriend. She couldn't bring herself to imagine looking at her beautiful Anne, stretched out in a coffin, dressed in clothing that she probably never wore. Her face would not be the one she kissed so many times. Her soft lips would be hard and most likely covered in red lipstick, something she would never wear. It wouldn't be her. She refused to have Anne's body in the casket be the last image she would ever have.

Beth began sobbing again. Her mind started to race, her thoughts were becoming erratic and obscure. She tried intensely to pull herself out of this dark cloud. Her heartache was excruciating, and the depression was sucking the life out of her. Just trying to think was overwhelming, but she tried hard to concentrate. Clarity came slowly at first, but then something suddenly struck her, as if someone had just punched her in the gut. Her mind came out of the fog. It was clear to her now…I'm not going to plan her funeral...I'm going to run for her instead. That's a promise I'm not going to break. She'd want me to. She'd be angry if I didn't. What was I thinking? I have no choice…I have to run for her. I promised her. Decision made, she would call the Stetson's after the meet and apologize.

CHAPTER FORTY-ONE

The Loneliest Mile

Beth had no more than an hour to get ready for the meet. There wasn't a second to spare. She threw water on her face, wiped the blood off her body, threw on a fresh T-shirt and shorts and ran to the sports complex.

The meet was well underway when she arrived. The stadium was filled but no one seemed to notice her when she entered. She headed straight for the locker room to change into her uniform. On her way, she noticed the hurdlers were starting. That meant the sprinters were next, and then the mile run. She had to hurry. The locker room was empty. She headed to Anne's locker instead of her own. She whizzed through the lock combination and pulled the door open. There it was…Anne's fresh track shirt, hanging defiantly before her. Beth gently lifted it off the hook. It looked lost without Anne's strong shoulders inside it. She rubbed the silkiness between her fingers, then put it up to her face to feel the softness. The clean smell reminded her of Anne. If she closed her eyes tight enough, she could imagine Anne standing next to her changing into that shirt. She could almost hear Anne telling her to hurry up and get changed or they would be late for the meet. Beth suddenly pulled off her own shirt and slipped Anne's jersey over her head. She was going to keep her promise…she was going to run for Anne.

As she ran from the locker room, she could see the milers on the side of the track, doing their final stretching before stepping onto the track to take their positions.

"Did you enter me?" Beth yelled to Coach Ryan as she ran towards her. Coach Ryan's expression was a combination of surprise and relief.

"Yes! Thank God! Where's Anne?" she hollered. Apparently, no one knew the tragic news about Anne. Beth could not bring herself to reveal the truth. It would do no good anyway. It would help no one.

"Something happened...she won't be coming. I'm running for her today," was all Beth could get out before her eyes started filling with tears. Coach Ryan was confused and concerned. The look on Beth's face was that of pain and desperation.

"Beth what's wrong?" Coach said nervously.

"I'm sorry..." Beth said crying, "I have to go now. I have a promise to keep."

Beth stepped onto the track to take her position in the lane next to Carol. She could clearly hear Liza and her friends cheering loudly. She couldn't look at them though, they would see her crying. Carol walked over and grasped Beth's hand. She looked into Beth's tear filled eyes. "Beth! What's going on? Are you all right?" She could see that Carol knew something was terribly wrong. Beth couldn't answer her though. She just stared at Carol.

"Beth what's wrong! Where's Anne?" Carol looked panicked.

"Runners please take your positions," a man directed before Beth had to explain. As she walked up to her spot, she could feel Carol still watching her. Beth couldn't look at her though, she was using every bit of power she had to focus on this race. She had to win. There was no other option. She knew State College's best runner, Brittany Spence, was in the lane next to her, and Trish Marie was on Carol's other side. They would be the ones most likely to beat her. Maybe even more so than Carol. Focus, focus, Beth repeated to herself. She ignored it when Brittany wished her good luck. She ignored the rude comments coming from the heckler in the stands. She ignored the supportive cheers coming from her friends. She could only think about one thing...winning. I'm keeping my promise Anne...I'm running for you, and I plan to win. I promise I will give it everything I've got. Those were Beth's last thoughts before the gun went off.

Beth pulled out fast to clear the crowd of runners and get an inside lane. The best she could manage was third, in back of both Brittany and Trish. Beth wasn't sure, but she thought Carol might be behind her. Beth increased her pace significantly within the first quarter mile. It was much faster than her usual pace, but it allowed her to pass both of State's runners and take the lead. She continued to accelerate until she was ahead by almost ten yards. This was completely contrary to her usual strategy. Coach Ryan didn't like it. She was hollering at Beth to slow down and follow the strategic running plan that was specifically designed for her and Anne. Beth disregarded the advice. She wouldn't even make eye contact. She had to trust her gut, she had to do it her way. Beth held the lead past the half mile mark. She could hear State's coach yelling to his runners, "Don't worry about her…let her burn herself out!" She heard another voice screaming, "Don't let her beat you Brittany!!! You're a true winner, now prove it!!!"

Beth's pace was taking its toll on her legs. They felt like they were starting to go numb. Her muscles began to lose force with each contraction. It didn't matter how hard she pushed herself. If her muscle fibers couldn't provide the power, she couldn't maintain the pace. Her third quarter showed it. As they started the last quarter, Coach Ryan yelled encouragingly at Beth to "Keep it up. You're doing great. You've got this Beth!" She didn't give any advice. She knew Beth was going to do it her way.

Beth's rivals were closing in. They were only a few yards away. The crowd was on its feet. Beth could hear their strides pounding the track just behind her. Beth gave it everything she had but she just couldn't go any faster. State's coach and fans were yelling with satisfaction as their runners pulled up next to Beth and passed her. Carol was amongst them.

"Please Beth! Get the fuck going!" Carol yelled at Beth as she passed her.

Beth knew she couldn't stay with them. Her muscles couldn't take it. They needed to rest for a moment. Much to the surprise of everyone, she eased up her pace even more. She fell further behind, but she quickly began to feel her well trained body starting to respond to the short rest. There wasn't much time left to catch up. Her throat burned and the sweat rolled off her face as she pushed her pace back up. She was closing in on them. but she could see the finish line at the end of the straight away. The thought that she had to do this for Anne, and couldn't fail her, kept repeating frantically through her mind. She poured out every ounce of energy her body had left to offer. She was running strictly on adrenalin now. Her kick became longer and powerful again. The muscles in her legs bulged with each stride. She passed Carol and pulled up next to Brittany and Trish. They ran shoulder to shoulder for several yards until Beth managed to pass them by less than half a stride. Beth's desperate face showed the emotional and physical strain. Her arms pumped furiously. She began praying for help. They were twenty yards from the finish line. Beth didn't think she could do it. She was ready to give up.

"Don't give up!!!" Carol screamed as loud as she could as she pulled up next to Beth's shoulder. Beth could see the finish line right in front of her, but it seemed a mile away. Her mind went blank as she closed her eyes, stuck out her chest and gasped in pain as her legs collapsed beneath her. She crashed violently down onto the track, tearing even more skin off of her already battered body. She rolled to a stop and laid there unable to move. She wasn't sure what had just happened.

"Beth…you did it," Carol said as she knelt down next to her and gently placed her hand behind Beth's head to help her to sit up. Others, including Coach Ryan and the athletic trainers came running over to help, but Carol waved them away. Beth could only look at Carol. No words would come out of her mouth. Carol moved in close to Beth and held her in her arms as Beth began to weep. Carol held her tighter as she whispered to her, "You won Beth...you won. Anne will be so proud of you."

Beth kept her head on Carol's shoulder as she sobbed, "She'll never know Carol, she'll never know."

"What do you mean Beth? Of course, she will," Carol said soothingly.

"She was in a car accident...she didn't make it."

"What? What do you mean she didn't make it?" Carol's face filled with fear. She looked directly into Beth's eyes.

"She died Carol...she died."

Carol said nothing, but the expression on her face spoke clearly...shock, devastation, and heartache. She pulled Beth tightly against her and rocked her. She tried not to cry but she couldn't stop the tears.

"Come on...come with me," Carol said as she pulled Beth up. "Let's get you to the locker room," she said as she placed Beth's arm around her shoulder and helped her up. They walked slowly off the track. Everyone, including the reporters, seemed to understand that they needed to be alone. Brittany and Trish offered their congratulations as Beth and Carol passed, but it went unheard.

The walk to the locker room was silent. Neither of them could manage to speak. When they reached the door, Beth released herself from Carol's arm and said, "I want to be alone for a little bit...will you stay here and make sure no one comes in?"

"Yes...of course. Are you sure you don't want me to help you? At least let me help you clean the cuts."

"No. I can do it. I'm sorry...I just need to be by myself."

"Okay Beth...I'll be right here if you need me," Carol said as she embraced Beth tightly. They held each other for several moments. It seemed that neither of them wanted to let go.

As the door closed behind Beth, the noise and excitement of the stadium were shut out. It was empty and quiet inside. As she walked to Anne's locker, her footsteps echoed off the metal lockers. She sat down on the bench in front of the locker and leaned her head back against the door. Her body was completely drained, and horribly beaten. She sat motionless. The sweat was still rolling down her face and dripping from her hair. She could taste its saltiness on her lips. She stared blankly at nothing. Her brain raced but nothing made sense. Finally, she stood and started to open Anne's lock. She didn't know if she wanted to see the inside again. The memories might comfort her, but they might devastate her too. She turned the dial on the lock and entered the combination, but the lock wouldn't open. She spun it and started over, but it still didn't open. After an unsuccessful third attempt, Beth punched her hand into the metal grating on the locker door. "Damn it!" She shouted furiously. "Fucking lockers…" she said as she sank back down on the bench and began to cry. Then she heard the locker room door squeak open and footsteps coming in her direction. "Shit," she said angrily to herself. Either Carol let someone in, or Carol was checking on her. She didn't want to see or talk to anyone. She just wanted to be alone. She looked for something to hide her reddened eyes. She grabbed a towel that was laying on the floor nearby and covered her face with it, as if she were absorbing her sweat. She could tell that the footsteps were coming down her aisle. The footsteps were soft, and the gate was slow. Beth kept her face hidden, hoping whoever it was would go away. The footsteps stopped. Beth felt the presence of someone kneeling down in front of her. They said nothing. Beth just wanted them to leave. There was a gentle tug on the towel. Beth picked up a faint but familiar fragrance. It made her heart race nervously.

"Congratulations Beth," a voice said softly. Beth's heart started pounding as she slowly lowered her towel and looked up disbelievingly into a pair of beautiful blue eyes.

"Anne?" Beth said in a whisper. She was speechless for a moment. She could only stare at her. Her mind was trying to make sense of this. It couldn't be true, but it was. "Anne!!!" Beth screamed, as she stood and threw herself into Anne's arms. "Oh my God! Oh my God!" Beth began to sob. "I thought you were dead…" Beth could barely get the words out. They held each other in a way that promised they would never separate.

"I'm okay…I'm here now," Anne said softly as she held Beth tight and rocked her in her arms. Beth tried to talk but nothing came out clearly. She was crying so hard she couldn't make it through a complete sentence. She got out the words, "telephone call", "car accident", and "dead".

"No…no…no," Anne seemed confused, but she tried to sooth Beth. "I'm fine. Someone lied to you. I would have been at the meet, but I got a call that the meet was canceled. I've been calling you, but you never answered or called me back. I went to your room when I got back, but you weren't there, so I went to the apartment. Liza left me a note saying she was going to the meet to cheer us on. I didn't understand what was happening. That woman told me that the meet had been canceled. I'm so sorry I wasn't here for you, but everything is going to be okay now. Don't cry. We're fine." Anne stroked Beth's hair and kissed her cheek. "I love you Beth. I love you so much," Anne whispered.

"I have to tell you…" Beth could only talk between sobs. "The woman that called said your parents wanted me to come to your house today, to help plan your funeral."

"What?" Anne's voice rose in disbelief. "What woman? This is so sick. How could anyone do something so horrible?"

"I'm sorry Anne. I didn't think I could live without you," Beth said as she started losing control. "I wanted to kill myself. I tried."

"Beth! What are you saying?" Anne said in a panic.

"I'm so sorry...I'm so sorry. I just wasn't strong enough. It hurt so badly. I didn't want to be here without you," Beth wept.

"I don't understand...did you try to kill yourself?"

"Yes."

"Oh my God Beth...no, no, please don't say that. Oh my God..." Anne cried out in shock as she began weeping.

They held onto each other so tight that neither of them could move. In this way, they shared their pain and their relief.

"I kept my promise to you though," Beth said as she pulled back and looked into Anne's watery eyes. "You made me promise that if you couldn't run for whatever reason, that I would have to run for you. I decided not to go plan your funeral so I could stay here and run for you. I did it Anne, I did it...I won it for you."

"I know you did, my little champion," Anne smiled and used her thumb to wipe the tears on Beth's face. "Carol told me. She was as shocked to see me as you were. She looked so upset and confused that she couldn't stop crying."

"She really helped me Anne," Beth said as she wiped away more tears. "She's one of the reasons I won. She took care of me when you couldn't."

"I told you she's a good person. You're both true champions."

Beth placed her head in Anne's neck and wrapped her arms tightly around her.

"Please don't ever let anything happen to you. I love you too much to make it without you."

"I can say the same to you. We have too much to look forward to. I'll love you forever...I promise."

Beth would be going to the National Championships soon, but Anne wouldn't be joining her. She no longer qualified because she missed the Divisional Championship. Anne's motivating presence would be absent from the racetrack. She wouldn't be running by Beth's side, and they wouldn't be crossing the finish line together. Beth would be running alone. Beth would be ready though, for the loneliest mile had already been won.

CHAPTER FORTY-TWO

EPILOGUE
What Happened?

A subsequent investigation determined that this unspeakable act was committed by the mother of Brittany Spence. For her part, Brittany knew nothing of what her mother had done. She was mortified by this atrocious act, but not completely surprised.

Her mother had been battling mental illness for a long time. As an only child, whose father died when she was eleven, Brittany had grown up a sole witness to her mother's unpredictable and misguided behaviors. Her mother's high IQ amplified her cleverness. When she used it inappropriately however, it became extremely dangerous, and caused chaos and heartbreak in Brittany's life.

Brittany was often embarrassed to be with her mother in public and begged her to get help. It was futile. Her mother denied anything was wrong. Brittany witnessed throughout high school and into college, how the untreated illness continued to worsen, and the irrational thoughts and behaviors that her mother exhibited, became more frequent.

Brittany told no one about what was going on, but she perceived that people knew something was wrong with her mother. Other parents, particularly at track meets, didn't sit near her, or attempt to engage her in conversation. Her mother was known for screaming at Brittany to "take down" or "destroy" her opponents. Brittany hoped fervently that her mother wouldn't show up to her events, but she always did. She was Brittany's biggest fan. Once, she told Brittany that she would do anything to make her only child a winner. That was the same day she made those dreadful calls. It seemed she could not differentiate between love and lunacy.

Apparently, Brittany's mother was determined to stop anyone from beating her beloved daughter at any cost. Keeping Beth and Anne off of the track that day was the only way to do it. It turned out that Mrs. Spence had called the athletic director's office claiming to be Anne's aunt. She explained there had been a family emergency and needed to get in touch with both Anne Stetson and her dear friend Beth Locke immediately. She would need the numbers listed in their records so she could locate them quickly. The concerned secretary didn't hesitate to provide her with the numbers. At least this part of her plan worked. She was lucky enough to catch Anne at her parent's home to tell her the meet had been canceled and to find Beth in her dorm room to notify her that Anne had been killed in a car accident. Her plan to keep Beth out of the race by sending her off to plan Anne's funeral didn't work, and it almost resulted in a far more tragic outcome.

As soon as Brittany found out what had happened, she made desperate attempts to apologize to Beth and Anne, for the pain and destruction her mother's scheme had caused. She called and wrote letters, blaming herself and asking for their forgiveness. She shared that her mother was now getting help, but she knew it was too late to take back the devastation already caused. She went to see them in person and could barely speak. She was overwhelmed with guilt and sobbed until Anne's hug slowed the tears and softened her pain.

Beth and Anne never sought her apology. They understood that Brittany wasn't responsible for her mother's behaviors and held no hard feelings against her. They accepted the apology only because they thought it would make Brittany feel better. This terribly divisive experience would eventually provide the three of them, the opportunity to grow closer.

The
Loneliest
Mile

Made in the USA
Middletown, DE
31 July 2021